ST. PETER'S FIASCO

Buona Fiesta
Cuzzin!!

:)

Kory Curcuru

ST. PETER'S FIASCO

The Perfect Storm Spoof

Kory Curcuru

Copyright © 2003 by Kory Curcuru.
Library of Congress Number: 2003094895
ISBN: Hardcover 1-4134-2138-5
　　　 Softcover 1-4134-2137-7

All rights reserved. No part of this book may be reproduced or transmitted in any form or by any means, electronic or mechanical, including photocopying, recording, or by any information storage and retrieval system, without permission in writing from the copyright owner.

This is a work of fiction. Names, characters, places and incidents either are the product of the author's imagination or are used fictitiously, and any resemblance to any actual persons, living or dead, events, or locales is entirely coincidental.

This book was printed in the United States of America.

To order additional copies of this book, contact:
Xlibris Corporation
1-888-795-4274
www.Xlibris.com
Orders@Xlibris.com
20616

CONTENTS

Glossary 17
Disclaimer 21
1 : Glosta, Mass., 19whateva 33
2 : Weird White People 101 44
3 : And Now a Word from Our Sponsor 56
4 : Off of the Island and Into the Streets 65
5 : The Scrotum Pole 70
6 : The Riggiz of the Road 82
7 : The Fuller Squish 89
8 : Unskinny Bop 112
9 : Tina Cafeena Talks 114
10 : St. Peter's Fiasco 119
11 : Me Cuzzin. Me No Understand 126
Post Script 131

THIS BOOK
IS DEDICATED
TO DRUNK MEN
EVERYWHERE
RISKING THEIR LIVES
CHASING FLAGS
AT THE ENDS OF
GREASED POLES

HALF-ASS PRAISE FOR ST. PETER'S FIASCO

"UNINSPIRED . . . almost sad in the sense that this never should have been written."
-Lawrence Faye Bran
Dean of English, Anglo A&M

"REGRETTABLE . . . you weren't supposed to see this."
-Dr. Imalu Scannon
Kory's live-in therapist

"EMBARRASSING . . . we're looking into serious-ass legal action."
-sole public statement issued by Curcuru family

"EVERCHANGING . . . it's a coaster *and* a doorstop!"
-Mary Muzzintuch, CEO
Mothers With Too Much Time

"HEY . . . I thought you had to be from out of town or over 70 to write a book about Gloucester?"
-Kory Curcuru

ST. PETER'S FIASCO
AKA
THE FULLER SQUISH

An Untrue Story
of Men Against
Themselves

PRODUCED, MIXED and ENGINEERED by
KORY CURCURU for
ANYONE LISTENING

EDITOR: (NONE BRAVE ENOUGH)
AGENT: (KNOW ANY GOOD ONES?)
CATERING: (UNITED NATIONS FLATBED
HANDOUTS)
MANAGEMENT: (FILL IN HERE)
COVER ART DESIGN: MICHAEL CUCURULLO
COVER ART TEXT: BIG ALLEN BEY

SPECIAL THANKS TO EVERYONE IN NORTHFIELD
and BARRE, VT, HINGHAM, NEWTON, BRIGHTON
and JAMAICA PLAIN, MA, ATLANTA, GA,
RIDGEWOOD, NJ, DILLON, CO and SOUTHFIELD, MI
OVER THE YEARS FOR WARM BEDS AND
COLD BEERS

EXTRA THANKS TO:
I'M WITH STUPID and SHIFT 8 IMPROV
WORLDWIDE
THE LADIES PROFESSIONAL BOWLING TOUR
THE SAN DIEGO CHARGERETTES
THE "BOYS IN VERMONT"
ALL FRIENDS and FAMILY (YES, BOTH SIDES)

AND EXTRA SPECIAL THANKS TO:
EVERYONE IN GLOUCESTER
FOR THE BACKBONE

KORY CURCURU USES AND RECOMMENDS THE
FOLLOWING EQUIPMENT:
CUSHY ROCKER/RECLINERS
HEADPHONES WITH MORE TREBLE THAN BASS
ABOUT 10% OF AN UNDERACHIEVING
HUMAN BRAIN

THE TEXT IN THIS BOOK IS PRINTED
ON PAPER FROM BABY TREES
HACKED DOWN BEFORE HAVING A CHANCE TO
BEAUTIFY THE COUNTRYSIDE

TWO SHOW PONIES WERE QUARTERED TO
PROVIDE THE GLUE FOR THIS BINDING

THE AUTHOR WOULD ALSO LIKE TO
ACKNOWLEDGE SOME PEOPLE
WHO WERE VERY IMPORTANT IN MAKING THIS
BOOK POSSIBLE:
THANKS KORY, YOU'RE GREAT.

FOR MORE INFO ON THE REDHEADED RIGHTS
MOVEMENT SEND PANTIES, PAPER MONEY OR
DEATH THREATS TO:
THE FULLER SQUISH
BOX 5502, MAGNOLIA, MA 01930

"It doesn't matter whether everyone gets it,
as long as the right people get it."

—Joel Hodgson
intergalactic visionary

"I know I ain't doin' much,
doin' nothin' means a lot to me."

—Bon Scott actual rock star

"You can go fug a fuggin'."

—Frankie Vermann
Boulevard fleet captain

GLOSTARY

(some words purposely misspelled
for phonetic reasons)

Bevalee—Beverly, Mass.
Boulevahd—Stacy Boulevard, Gloucester's aorta and main thoroughfare
CATA—Cape Ann Transportation Authority; public busing
Cocaine Lane—I'm not touching this one
the Cut—drawbridge along the Boulevard on Western Avenue
Cuz, Cuzzin—what every young Glostaman aspires to be
the Factory—unaffectionate term for Gloucester High School
5-4's—percosets
fuggin' or fu'in—take a guess
Gee-fi?—throwaway Sicilian jive; non sequitur for non-thinkers
Glochick—Glosta girl (they're fair and dandy)
Glosta—how real people from Gloucester pronounce *Gloucester*
the Harbor—Gloucester Harbor
Horribles Parade—costume parade held around Fourth of July
Keepahs—females most sought after by Cuzzins
kweah—queer
mug-up—coffee break
packy—liquor store
pitchaz—pictures
Portagee—Americanized Portuguese immigrant
resinators—remnants of previous bong hits lit for quick toke

Schoolies—any very young, very available female
Scrotum Pole—the Boulevard pecking order
seine boat—kinda like an Italian canoe, people race in it during Fiesta
shotgun(ner)—the passenger or passenger seat
shoulder-tap—asking an adult to buy alcohol as you hide from cops
squid—condom
the Statue—the historic Man-at-the-Wheel monument
steak swing—any gathering, party or bar overwhelmingly occupied by males
suntin'—something
sword fight—(see steak swing)
'Vahd—the Boulevard
wickit (or wigged)—wicked
Xtasy—psychoactive designer drug, slightly more effective than One-A-Day vitamins
zazeets—Sicilian slang for Italian sausage with peppers and onions
Zippa—carnival ride; a Fiesta favorite
zucci (or zoochi)—wharf rat

ST. PETER'S FIESTA

GLOUCESTER, MA 01930
PROGRAM OF EVENTS

THURSDAY

8:00-11:00 p.m.—ENTERTAINMENT—Sybil the One-Woman Trio

FRIDAY

4:45 p.m.—WOMEN'S SEINE BOAT RACE OPEN INVITATION GREASY POLE
6:00 p.m.—THE PARADISE BAND—Concert
8:30 p.m.—FORMAL OPENING—A Candlelight Procession will lead St. Peter's statue to Fiesta Altar
9:30 p.m.-12:00 a.m.—ENTERTAINMENT—Slow, Sad Violin Music

SATURDAY

3:00 p.m.—CHILDREN'S GAMES—at Beach Court Watermelon/Pie Eating, Egg Throwing

4:45 p.m.—SPORTS EVENTS—Pavilion Beach Seine Boat Races, Greasy Pole Contest
8:00 p.m.-12:00 a.m.—ENTERTAINMENT—Music by DJ "7 Cornrow Tommy" & Tom Callahan Jumps for Cash

SUNDAY

10:15 a.m.—MASS OF ST. PETER—St. Peter's Park Seymour Smallboise, Archbishop of Boston Reverend Slick, St. Ann Church Mixed Choir
12:00 p.m.—RELIGIOUS PROCESSION FOLLOWING THE SOLEMN CELEBRATION OF MASS
3:00 p.m.—BLESSING OF THE FLEET—SEYMOUR SMALLBOISE at Stacy Boulevard; Individual Boat Blessings to follow
4:45 p.m.—SPORTS EVENTS—at Pavilion Beach Seine Boat Races, Greasy Pole Contest
6:30 p.m.—Children's Pinata Contest—Pascucci Court
7:30 p.m.-11:30 p.m.—The Guy Cloutman Orchestra—Concert
9:00 p.m.—AWARDS CEREMONY—Trophies awarded to winners of the Sports Events
10:00 p.m.—GRAND FIREWORKS DISPLAY—Gloucester Harbor
11:00 p.m.—RAFFLE PRIZE DRAWINGS—at the Bandstand
11:30 p.m.—CLOSING PROCESSION—St. Peter's Statue will again be returned to the Shrine at St. Peter's Club

DISCLAIMER

This is a take-off of Sebastian Junger's *The Perfect Storm*. But it has nothing to do with a fishing accident, or the people in it, or fishing at all. This is simply a story about other people in Gloucester told in the same vein as Junger's bestseller.

The success of *The Perfect Storm* put my hometown Gloucester, Massachusetts in the limelight. It inspired a major motion picture. It inspired me too. It also inspired a junior high school class field trip to the Crow's Nest, the local watering hole featured in the novel and movie. I think it's sweet for kids to return to the place where some of them were actually conceived.

The story I wrote is about what young guys from Gloucester think and do from high school until they're too embarrassed to attend keg parties. And while I do go off on wild tangents and take instances to the extreme, everything that occurs in this book *has* happened, *does* happen, and *will continue to happen*. That's beyond debate.

•

This book has two titles: *St. Peter's Fiasco* and *The Fuller Squish*. The first title, the one eventually found on the cover, was done for commercial purposes. It's an obvious play on St. Peter's Fiesta, the popular four-day holiday held annually in my hometown, and the hope is that title will attract tourists and lazy shoppers who have heard of Gloucester's version of Mardi Gras.

To me, the book will forever be *The Fuller Squish*. That's what I named it from its inception nearly five years ago, and how I will always refer to it. I'll explain later . . .

Now—a little history. The legendary Spanish nobleman Don Juan was famous for his many seductions and dissolute life. Giovani Jacopo Casanova, the Italian adventurer and writer, also had a reputation for having numerous amorous adventures. The yarns of lustful rakes like Don Juan and Casanova are emulated but rarely duplicated by daydreaming men worldwide, especially in this old fishing port. Here and today, the men are not known as Casanovas but "Cuzzins," a macho twist on the blood-relative word "cousin." Cuzzins, or Cuzzes even, are crawling everywhere, and Gloucester seems to be the global headquarters for this mass fraternity. If ever in the bowels of Glosta, surrounded by honest-to-goodness Glostamen, choking alive in a cloud of cheap cologne, one will undoubtedly hear this phrase more often than a sick seagull's caw: "What's up Cuzzin?" Or, in shorter terms, "S'up Cuz?" It's the city's official motto. It's even printed in Latin across the crest of Gloucester's coat of arms: *Quo Fit Cusinus?* Would you like to know more about the thinking and mating patterns of the wild and woolly Bare-Chested Gloucester Cuzzin? Me too! Keep reading!

•

Recreating the last hours of five local lads who disappeared in Greater Boston was easy. The entire story is based on the experiences of several legendary Cuzzins, all friends and acquaintances. I'm a lifelong resident. So I figure I've essentially written a book for and about people who grew up just like me.

If I were too bored to create an explanation of what happened aboard the doomed Camaro, I'd commiserate with buddies and recount similar situations we endured. The difference being, of course, we came home. Those experiences certainly provide a dead-on description of what the five Cuzzins in the *IROC-Z* went through, complained about, and probably suffered.

In short, I've written as fake an account as possible of something I never really thought through. It's that childish attitude that made it easy to write, and I hope, to read. As far as spoofing *The Perfect Storm*—relax. I've purposely misspelled names and bungled facts. Made up the ending, too.

•

Anything in direct quotes was recorded in a formal interview with a fictitious person. All dialogue is based on stories from genuine lady-lovin' Cuzzins, and appears in dialogue form without quotation marks. Technical discussions of bedding astonishingly overweight women are based on my own fearless investigations. I don't wanna talk about it.

My everlasting sexual experience of Fiesta Eve was limited to sobbing quietly while watching scrambled Cinemax on my parents' cold kitchen floor. As I reached the apex of my intimacy I realized to my horror the family dog, a black and white cocker spaniel, was spying on me. So I threw the remote control at Pepper. Without even knowing it, I had begun to turn into a jerk.

•

One thing: This is not written in proper English. I am not a proper Englishman. I'm an improper American. I don't say things like, "Look Guv, I stepped on me foot. And, blymie, there's a bit of hair in me eyes." I say things like, "Chicken pot pie" and "First and ten" and "Where's my gun?"

As far as the names of the characters go: I mostly stuck with types of food and pastas for last names. They're Italian. They're recognizable. And it's not worth making the mistake of misspelling a common name from around here. Even though each name is listed a thousand times in the local phone book, you'd be surprised how often some out-of-towner shows up and scrambles all the vowels. The other names are derogatory names friends give other friends. Nothing new there.

Two names, however, deserve further explanation. The last name of Tony and Tulip Baloney is actually spelled Bologna. It's just pronounced Baloney.

The name of the Cadillac fleet captain is the Americanized name of Francisco Virmani, the Sicilian balladeer. Virmani came to the States at the turn of the twentieth century and performed in vaudeville clubs nationwide as Frankie Vermann. The name change was easy for Francisco since, like most immigrant entertainers, he was ashamed of his heritage anyway. Upon learning of Virmani, I also read about another Frankie Vermann, this one a Scottish shepherd who invented elasticized legbands to ease the strains of shearing sheep. Both Vermanns died in 1933. Both died of latent syphilis. The coincidence was too cool to pass.

•

Yes, the Glostary is incomplete. I thought *listening* to the accent was hard. Try writing in it. Anyway, you'll live.

•

Another thing: Gloucester, or as I like to call it, the People's Republic of Dunkin' Donuts, is a great city. Honestly. I played Little League and beer softball here. I've wondered aloud when the downtown meter maids needed to be returned to East Berlin. I've thrown up Jello shots and malt liquor before high school dances. I'd like to do it all again someday. And the Fiesta rocks. Best time of year.

Both sides of my family live here. That's a lot of Curcurus (pronounced "KOOK-a-roo"). It's that way for most Gloucesterites. This is a quirky island. I'm talkin' Twin Peaks quirky. Come visit us sometime, drop off your daughters, then leave.

•

Speaking of family and friends, I've done more than my fair

share of mooching off them all these past few years. They waited patiently after I quit school and started doing stand-up. They waited some more when I quit stand-up to write a book. They're waiting now that I'm in improv. And waiting . . . and waiting . . . and waiting . . .

Originally, I thought I would use this space to explain all the shit that happened between leaving school and finishing this book. First there was the stand-up career. Know what I can't stand? Stand-up comedy and stand-up comics. So I became one. I could tell you all about the failed attempts to produce a CD with two different companies. Or the nights I spent sleeping in North Station. Or the failed attempt to start a radio career I never wanted to begin anyway. I could tell you how my first novel, written longhand with pencil on computer paper, was actually returned to me in a shoebox (casket). Or about my attempts, or lack thereof, at finding a real job. Or what it's like to live without a car or an apartment or health insurance or a dental plan. Or the fact that I still can't tie a tie or make a pot of coffee or drive a stick shift.

On the other hand, I could tell you what it's like to show up at a bar at 10:30, have a couple beers, tell a dozen jokes, and get paid a day's wage. Or about quitting jobs so I could travel cross-country with a buddy or watch a concert a country away. Or about my famous luggage: See me with my blue and grey Kennex tennis bag, I'm staying the weekend. See me with my Boston Bruins heavy equipment bag, stock the fridge.

I never would have become a fifty-cent millionaire without the support of a few people who, aggravated as they may be with my laziness, can't bring themselves to say no on account of my cute smile and infectious company. They are, in no particular order: Peter Banacos, Alexis Dekel, Matt Turnbull, Jamie Duprey, Jesse Duprey, Jason Lemery, and Keith and Valerie Brickey. Dan Cooper, Aaron Rose, Anthony Taormina and Tom Callahan. John Zannis, Todd Olsen, Mike Brazis, and Tim Dow. Allen Bey, Mike Cucurullo and Andy Ellinghaus. Guy Cloutman and Brian Watson, and all families and significant others of those listed. Also, raise a glass high for Dick and Barbara Wilson of the Wilson

Winter Retreat. And of course, a special nod of thanks to Dana and Joanne and the staff at Curcuru Bed and Breakfast in Magnolia.

Back to the *Squish*.

•

I know Gloucester. In researching this book, I was actually born and raised here.

Some of you may find the views expressed in this book controversial. But I'm sure that if George Clooney were to say them on the silver screen between layups at State Fish Pier, you'd eat 'em up. So look for someone else to tar and feather in front of City Hall.

•

You're right: This should be required reading for every pupil in the Gloucester public school system.

Right again: There should be a *Fuller Squish* scholarship established for C-minus students who couldn't care less about what their textbooks tell them.

•

One last thing: The term *Fuller Squish* has been around since June 1986. It was not until I needed the perfect title for this book that its connotation became naughty. But back in '86, I was in my final days at Milton L. Fuller Middle School. And it was about that time that testosterone began to do strange things to this body I now call a man's. There must have been 200 other preteens like myself at Fuller trying to deal with Mother Nature's witchery.

One release we commonly practiced was to carry our books around in hockey gloves, find an unsuspecting fourth-grader, drop our gloves, and beat him senseless. When that became too boring, we would block the doorways as the entire student body reentered the building from recess. This resulted in Altamont-style mosh pits. In time, *Fuller Squishes* began to pop up like pimples. Bathrooms and classrooms and hallways and cafeterias would be filled with children screaming for dear life. It was absolute mayhem.

The *Fuller Squish* lasted for years.
The scarring should last forever.

•

No, I'm not a professional cartographer, but thank you.
Yes, I should receive a free Camaro.

Thanks—Kook

Cast of Characters

Johnny Ziti
IROC-Z crewman

Tina Cafeena
Ziti's Glochick

Sal Rigatoni
Ziti's pal, *IROC-Z* crewman

Vito Ditalini
32-year-old keg veteran, *IROC-Z* coolerman

Tony Baloney
captain of the *IROC-Z*

Goita
prominent Gloucester slumlord

Petey Meatballeyes
lifelong friend of Tony, *IROC-Z* shotgunner

Bobby Zucci
original *IROC-Z* owner

Tulip Baloney
Tony's ma, Bobby Zucci's live-in girlfriend

Lorenzo Pimento
captain of 3/4 ton Bigfoot *America*

Frankie Vermann
captain of Cadillac *Seville 1*

Mad Dog
Seville 1 crewman

Chinstrap Calzone
Factory football legend

Joe Tomatoes
hopeful Cuz-to-be

Yo-Yo OneNut
friend of Ziti's, hopeful Cuz-to-be

Totebag
member of Glosta boy-band 4EVA

Headgear
member of Glosta boy-band 4EVA

D.L.S.H.
member of Glosta boy-band 4EVA

Velveeta
Ditalini's criminally underage Glochick

Perri Oxide
Joe Tomatoes's Glochick

and introducing Meester Joe as
Johnny's ding-dong

WHAT HAPPENS WHEN FIVE CUZZINS IN AN IROC GO OVER THE BRIDGE THE NIGHT BEFORE FIESTA?

1

Glosta, Mass., 19whateva

Thick patchy fog clings, hovers, recedes, then disintegrates entirely from Gloucester Harbor in early morning. When sunshine spits diamonds along the watertop, one can see footlong wharf rats run amok on Tenpound Island. Yellow city trucks crank spastically along Western Avenue, pausing to collect trash barrels beside the Boulevard, looking for places to hide until mug-up. Cracked sidewalks lead to rickety benches and seedless thatches of dirt; a perfect setting for dogs to squat and drop moonrocks. Cackling seagulls spackle the coastline with whites and greys. A gentle bullet-colored current nuzzles the Pavilion Beach shore, leaving foamy wetness and the odd syringe in its wake. Above it all, the sea green Man-at-the-Wheel squints with concern. Behind his haunting backside are the homes of his city: some beautiful, some adequate, some downright wretched.

In one of the holes, up the weather-beaten porch, behind asbestos walls, and into a $1400-a-month second-floor apartment, Johnny Ziti is sh'faced. There are video games and clothes strewn all over the floor. And though he doesn't know it, Johnny's shirt is streaked with special sauce. The stain is dangerously close to a golden barracuda pendant dangling from a rope-thick chain around his neck. Johnny goes nowhere without his fish.

Next to Johnny is his girlfriend. She has peroxide-blonde hair that on a good day can scrape the stratosphere, a nose that could hook a marlin, and a wet cardboard personality. She has a strong Glosta accent and a stronger affinity for cheap cigarettes. She's not ugly, just typical. She spends her summer evenings walking the two or three miles between ice cream stores. We'll call her Tina Cafeena.

Their master futon is below a picture window that overlooks Western Avenue, the Cut Bridge traffic, and the Harbor.

Fog still cuddles the breakwater. At Stacy Boulevard, back between the Statue and the walkway towards Pavilion Beach is where the nightlife walks, where cars and trucks shuttle creatures after sundown and make this town alive. During the day it's where older people walk and younger ones jog, where vendors hawk footlongs with all the fixings. It's where countless historic monuments are erected at an alarming pace.

Aside from many marked and dedicated benches and stones, there's the ancient Man-at-the-Wheel statue and the modern Fisherman's Wives monument. They define the Boulevard, and are the most photographed pieces of Gloucester by tourists and residents alike. Gloucester loves its photogenic monuments. So much so, that the city is already planning the construction of two more memorials, just the amount needed to fill what's left of the Boulevard. The first proposal, an iron-cast display of people standing in front of a monument, is already on the planning board. The second, an iron-cast display of people pointing and staring at people standing in front of a monument, happens to be on my planning board. Hey, they beat strip malls.

Goita used to jog, then walk this very path. And even now, so many years and so many footlongs later, she calls Gloucester home. In fact, dozens of families call Goita's Gloucester homes their homes too. Goita's a slumlord. She owns the three-story dump Johnny Ziti and Tina Cafeena live in. Out-of-town contractors with no vested interest in the community made dozens of buildings like Goita's years ago. Out-of-town contractors still work in Gloucester today, though now they're usually hired by the city to ruin its public schools. Goita hasn't hired an accredited plumber or handyman in her life but still manages to charge outrageous rates for rental. Her building rises over the Man-at-the-Wheel's shoulders, facing south.

(The Man-at-the-Wheel, by the way, is Gloucester's most noticeable landmark. Some of you may recognize his likeness to the Gorton's fisherman. Gorton's is the famous frozen seafood company based in Gloucester. Gorton's is a lot like the nuclear power plant in *The Simpsons*. Half the city works there, like it or not. The Gorton's fisherman is a hale and hardy seafarer and, as depicted in all those fishsticks commercials on television, one annoyingly happy and proud white dude. It's funny, because most of the fishermen I know are scrawny little immigrants with unemployment checks in one hand and cheap booze in the other. But whatever sells breaded mackerel, I guess.)

•

We're warming up now, aren't we?

•

It's way before noon and Johnny Ziti is slow to rise. He has super-slick black hair covering his body, a loose Gold's Gym tanktop so his muscles can breathe, and stubble that could grate parmesan. Johnny's been shaving since grade school. In a few short hours, he'll be all dolled up and rolling around in his dream machine, a breathtaking ocean-blue 1987 IROC-Z Camaro. There's a four-day fiesta looming, and the way Johnny sees it, women are gonna swarm to his car like bugs to a Blowpop. A foghorn somewhere outside moans. Johnny Ziti slides a vest over his tanktop. He's always looking for a fling. Flings make great stories.

Johnny and Tina scrape resin from a bong and stretch their copper-skinned bodies. Resinators are a great way to start the day. Resinators, coffee, and pre-packaged sandwiches. The screen accidentally pops from the front door as they slowly walk to the mini-mart just down the street. Roast beef and mayonnaise wrapped in cellophane goes for four bucks, which is a pretty good poke into Tina's tip money. And that's before cigarettes.

Johnny and Tina stagger to the spot on the Boulevard where kids migrate. Some are already here, drinking rum and milk from plastic keg cups. A buddy of Johnny's named Sal Rigatoni is wiping white paste from his tongue, still shaking the cobwebs from last night. "'Sup Cuz?" asks Rigga. Johnny offers a smoke. Rigga is tall and gangly, though it doesn't keep him from flaunting his chest. Can Rigga bench-press a broomstick? Hard to tell. His hair, when correctly managed, is short and spiky. The spiked tips are frosted blonde. Rigga could pass for a woodland pixie if he weren't like every other macho jackass his age.

The *IROC-Z* only comes out at night, so the three pile into Tina's 1982 Plymouth hatchback and head to Rigga's for showers and gelling. They circle back to the Boulevard and nab Vito Ditalini, a 32-year-old keg party veteran and fellow IROC driver. It's way before the crack of noon, and they're heading to the packy.

Vito Ditalini is a lifelong resident of Gloucester. He has curly, moistened, soccer-style hair and piano-key teeth three shades too white. He's a big boy and has tattoos of animals he's never seen, women he's never slept with, and foreign symbols he couldn't possibly explain. He has an obnoxious but hot teenage girlfriend who sticks to him like a barnacle. His ex-wife is a complete basketcase who never gets off his back. Vito's current love is on the same crazytrain. Ditalini needs to buy wine coolers for his girl's friends, so Tina brings the guys to a liquor store. Funny thing about Gloucester: No matter what part of town you're in, you're practically surrounded by packies. There really *is* no reason to leave the island.

Along the way they pass the Blackburn Tavern, where white people go to hear other white people play the blues; Old Timer's Tavern, where white people go to hear other white people play rap; and the House of Mitch, where everybody goes to see what life is like on Mars. They walk around the packy looking for specially flavored wine coolers: Peach Edgar Hoover, Two-Ton Grape, Cinnamon Goo. A buddy's mom is working behind the counter.

"Do I wanna know who *these* ah foh?" she asks, surveying the bottles.

"Nope, you don't," says Vito.

She pokes the register and notices Johnny's shirt.

"*Someone* went to Chick's last night," she points out.

"Yah, supah roast beef," says Johnny, failing to conceal his embarrassment. "Killa fuggin' grub!" He acts cool, but he's red about the head like the dink on a dog.

•

Whether St. Peter's Fiesta is coming or not, young men and women who flock to the West End are expected at the Boulevard every weekend. Once there, they adhere to the unspoken pecking order that has existed for generations. Inexperienced boys, that is, those without driver's permits, sit on benches with their mouths shut. Some skateboard, or rollerblade, or juggle, or whatever it is kids whose dads never played catch with them do. Older guys harass tourists passing by, seriously compare the aftertastes between Busch and Busch Lite, then suck down Tic-Tacs and pal around with beat cops. Girls mull and graze back and forth on Western Avenue, led by an extraordinary caravan of baby strollers. (There are usually more wheels on the sidewalk than in the avenue.) They openly dream about Hollywood lifestyles talentless middle-aged men script for preteens.

Tina knows everyone at the Boulevard. They smoke the same brand, flicking ash over the sea wall, and loiter in front of the same Main Street stores. This was precisely the scene the night Tina met Johnny.

•

The herd was out early that unremarkable evening, posing

and posturing. A fleet of vehicles, engines idling and stereos blasting, made Western Avenue nearly impassable. Pockets of kids wandered aimlessly for hours; complaining about their families, bitching of how little there is to do in Gloucester, bragging about how much they'll do when they're out of Gloucester. As long as weather permits, this happens every single day on the Boulevard, tick-tock, like a clock.

Despite the night's hoopla, time elapsed drowsily, inch by inch. Suddenly, as if from a dream, an aspirin-yellow Pontiac Firebird made a screeching U-turn in front of the Cut, snatching the attention of the throng, roaring to a thunderous stop before the Statue. Circles of awestruck people surrounded the car. Not one person dared to make a sound. The passenger-side window descended slowly, magically. Behind it bearing a cool grin, the Devil's grin, sat the sharpest sonofabitch a Glochick could lay her bloodshot eyes upon.

His shades cost as much as his haircut, which cost as much as his gold chain. Tina Cafeena's heart began to pump. She knew he was looking at her. The mysterious man lifted his shades, and a connection was made. Tina was drawn to the man, the car, the shades, that scruff. Johnny Ziti.

•

Tina recently separated from her high school sweetheart. They had been together since freshman year and were unanimously voted Class Couple. Eight hours after graduation, they split. Unattached, Tina became a hot commodity. She began floating around the Boulevard.

Johnny was a stud in training. He put entire paychecks from fishing into rent, clothing, and a gym membership. As soon as he and Tina locked eyes, it was as if the two shared the same brain. They were each other's property now.

Heroin can be stored safely in the stomachs of haddock, and short-tail lobsters can be stolen from illegal pots off the Magnolia coast, so Johnny had a little financial cushion, so to speak. He is able to absorb Tina's leeching and pays Goita rent for the upcoming summer in advance. Perhaps now, Goita for once might kick in for a cockaroach trap.

As luck would have it, the night Johnny and Tina met, they ran into local legend Tony Baloney, a Cuz with a rap sheet as thick as a driver's manual. Tony couldn't drive anymore. Damn state wouldn't let him. But he still owned an IROC, and Johnny Ziti was still just a passenger in a Pontiac. A deal was struck: Johnny got the IROC while Tony worked out his problems. But Johnny is simply a phone call away if Tony needs a lift.

•

And that's exactly what happens as Johnny stands in line at the packy. Tony calls. He wants to hit the malls. "That's crazy talk!" yells Tina. "Those malls ah ova ten miles away!" Tina can scream, but Johnny Ziti has tuned her out.

This is the watershed moment of his young life. Not only are he, Ditalini, Rigatoni and Baloney leaving Gloucester for the day, but Johnny will drive to the mall in an IROC.

First things first though. Tina has to get the boys out of the packy and back to the apartment. Although unsure how her new boyfriend will handle his first day-trip off the island, Tina welcomes the opportunity to spend the afternoon rehearsing dance numbers she's created for the July Fourth weekend's Horribles Parade. The clamshack she waitresses at sponsors the grandest float each year. While the restaurant owner waves robotically from the front of a flatbed truck, waitresses dressed like menu specials prance about and toss plastic clams filled with candy and gift certificates to onlookers. As Miss $6.99 Squid Platter, Tina is director of choreography, naturally.

•

Camaros are fully loaded babe magnets because their figures are so sleek and curvy. They must be constantly, meticulously pampered. They are too precious to risk cleaning at a commoner's car wash. Floormats must be shaken and vacuumed, dashboards swabbed with soft cloth, upholstery moisturized, windows blowdried, hubcaps and fenders buffed, the body waxed and whispered to. Under the hood, radiators are flushed, engines cleaned, carburetors convusted, transmissions brabled and rebrabled, fanbelts trillied, and batteries batterized.

Glochicks follow Camaros like soldiers in formation, around the Boulevard and Back Shore, past Long, Good Harbor and Wingaersheek Beaches, and on to the gym, the YMCA, the ball fields, and the finer shopping and tourists traps Gloucester has to offer. IROCs lie low during the day. Prowling is for nighttime. Some IROCs do go as far away from the island as the Liberty Tree Mall or Peabody Shopping Center, great spots for little girlies. Others get to strip joints on Route 1 or even Boston. But these are rare occurrences. IROCs out of Gloucester are like fish out of water.

IROC drivers aren't your average gas and go commuter. To them, the Camaro is an extension of their being. It's the personality they'll never have. How it drives *is* as important as how it looks and sounds. Honestly, give IROC drivers credit. They invest time and money to learn what it is to sit behind the tinted power windows of a magnetic sports vehicle. They have been passengers before, plankton on the Boulevard food chain. They grew up watching cheerleaders walk promptly past vans with custom paint jobs of mountaintops to pounce on Camaros. The only other vehicles that hold a candle to IROCs are rugged Bigfoot pickups. They are like sister ships. But don't fool yourself, Camaros are kings of the fleet.

The best captains keep their machines impeccably maintained. And Tony Baloney's IROC is immaculate. He bought the car from his mother's boyfriend, Bobby Zucci, a man known well around Cape Ann. An aggressive dealer and mechanic, Zucci's been involved with almost every IROC that has passed through Gloucester. (It's said his name appears somewhere on every IROC's papers. In fact, in some circles captains call IROCs "Rat Rockets," after Zucci.) His expertise apparently rubbed off on

Tony. "No one gets in or out of the fuggin' cah 'til I open the door," Cap'n Baloney famously barks to his crew. And who can argue? When Tony parks on the Boulevard, only the choicest Glochicks lean into his open windows.

It takes a special man to devote a few hours a day away from the mirror or tanning salon, especially during Gloucester's lonely, lonely, lonely winters. But the compensation for such hard work is what Cuzzins call the summer harvest. Each time a car picks up a girl, or tears a patch on Western Ave., the whole city notices. The smell and trail of burned rubber is the trademark of the Zuccis, Baloneys, and soon, Johnny Ziti. Imagine the response that ocean-blue IROC will get on the last Thursday in June, the first day of the four-day St. Peter's Fiesta.

•

Johnny Ziti has left Gloucester for the day. Tina Cafeena is with her clamshack coworkers at the Factory parking lot, working on new routines. This is the distraction from her boyfriend's voyage she so desperately needs.

The Cut on Western Avenue and the Highway Bridge are all that connects the bulk of Gloucester to mainland Massachusetts. Both bridges cross the voluminous Annisquam River. Between routines, Tina pictures the guys circling the rotary, making the slow climb up the Highway Bridge on Route 128 South. She swears she hears Tony ask for gas money. Luckily for Tina, rehearsal momentarily sweeps her away.

As quick as lightning, the girls synchronize steps to a medley of Top 40 favorites. They begin, under the ominous drone of Duran Duran's synthesized intro to *Hungry Like The Wolf*, by slowly blossoming from giant styrofoam takeout containers. When the beat rechannels to the bad-ass thunderbolt bass of Young MC's *Bust A Move*, the dancers strike Vogue-like poses and karate stances. Their costumes exude individuality. Caramel popcorn glued to parkas seems fitting for batter-dipped entrees, as do the sequin-coated, bulging whiffleball eyes of the catfish and red snapper. Miss Filet o' Salmon's heartbreaking egg-laying pantomime, (done hauntingly to Madonna's *Papa Don't Preach* by shaking pockets full of white gumballs into the empty spare tire reservoir of the flatbed), leads perfectly to the performance's peak. Tina's finishing touch this year, her signature move from her days as a peewee cheerleader, is an elaborate flourish of confetti buckets passed and dumped amongst the dancers as they gleefully retrace steps and close the lids of their styrofoam homes. The confetti represents tartar sauce.

The girls are energetic and focused, and despite Miss $5.95 Clam Roll arriving 20 minutes late, rehearsal sails smoothly. Regrettably, Miss Shrimp Bucket and Miss Super Codwich aren't speaking to each other. But then again, Miss Shrimp Bucket and Miss Super Codwich *never* speak to each other. In the frenzy of the day, Tina fails to realize it's almost sundown.

•

Tina scurries down Centennial Avenue nearing the Harbor, unaware of the trail of paper-mache coleslaw strands in her wake. She notices the familiar aqua sparkle of an IROC in Goita's driveway. Flying into the apartment, she finds Tony Baloney, Sal Rigatoni, Vito Ditalini and, yes, Johnny Ziti playing video games, surrounded by overstuffed bags from several laughable clothing stores of the North Shore. Tina Cafeena catches her breath, pops open a raspberry wine cooler and slips into Johnny's old varsity jacket. Her man has returned.

They'd been gone two hours at the mall and taken a week's worth of pay. To Cuzzins, fashion comes and goes like the tide. It is difficult to assess how everyone made out until the guys hit downtown. If someone standing in line for Reggae Night at the Madfish Grill is wearing a similar shirt, backup clothing may be required. Nevertheless, a trip to the mall is a trip to the mall: A very happy occasion. The Cuzzins were forced to be choosy with purchases. IROCs have limited baggage space. In the end though, the gentlemen stockpile new shoes, silky shirts and vests, sandals, sportswear, and more shades. They also stop in a couple jewelry stores, are unimpressed, and resign to buying cheap cigars for the drive.

More importantly for Johnny Ziti, his first venture off the island has been a rousing success. So much so, he and the Cuzzins quietly contemplate a more challenging excursion to Boston. They will undoubtedly be staying put in Gloucester the next few weeks for the Fiesta and Fourth of July celebrations, so a big night outside Cape Ann will be a great excuse for getting dressed for strange ladies and showcasing the Camaro.

•

Other friends arrive at the apartment, join in the video games, begin drinking, drugging and critiquing clothing. Bobby Zucci makes a rare cameo, looking to collect payments owed him by Tony. Before mental preparation for the night commences, the men have other business to attend to: Tracking girlfriends, icing alcohol, rolling joints, eating . . . Not to mention comparing prices of other available drugs: painkillers, coke, Xtasy. And we haven't got to personal grooming yet.

That's still hours away. In the apartment presently, spirits and spirit imbibing are running high, for everyone except Tina Cafeena. Not only is she but one girl in a sea of men, (a scene more typical in Gloucester than boiling whitecaps), but Johnny is not talking to her. Last night, Johnny and Tina sponged liquor with sandwiches at Chick's Roast Beef, a late night joint near the police station. Tina threw a tantrum and lost shredded meat on Johnny's tanktop.

"He forgot his shirt was on undah his vest," Tina Cafeena laments. "He ditn't realize it 'til he got to the mall. He's wickit fuggin' pissed."

The spat between the young lovers would play an important role in Johnny Ziti's decision to leave Gloucester the night before Fiesta, a truly blasphemous thought. But Johnny has felt the fine leather interior of Tony's IROC on his body. For the first time in his life, he feels alive.

2

Weird White People 101

More than half a century ago, the urbanization of Gloucester began with construction of the A. Piatt Andrew (Highway) Bridge. Until then, undeserving heirs of the Old Yankee Rich were forced to travel through rougher nearby neighborhoods like Beverly Farms and Manchester-by-the-Sea if they hoped to launch their daddy's yachts for the weekend.

Anyhoo:

It was developed chiefly to increase the trade of goods and services to and from Gloucester and throughout the booming area of Route 128 leading to Boston known as the North Shore. The construction of the Bridge coincided with burgeoning social and economic upheaval brought to Cape Ann by Baby Boomers, America's first generation to completely ignore the generations preceding and succeeding their own. Oddly enough however, the Bridge, an ugly ode to modern construction with its imposing arc rainbowing over the Annisquam River hundreds of feet below, served to *dis*connect Gloucester from mainland Massachusetts as it did to link it. Immediately following its opening, the Bridge became the focal point of several unexplainable occurrences, mystical and spooky, that has had an undeniable effect on the island-city to this day.

One such instance involves the story of an out-of-luck

fisherman returning from another unsuccessful expedition. After gaining port in the midst of night, with nothing more than scaly hands and a tacklebox of pride, he wraps a coil of wires in the engine room of his 35-foot vessel. As he walks from the wharf, his ship slowly ignites, and flames soon lick the lemony moon above the Harbor. In moments, the ocean swallows the only life the old fisherman knew. He never looks back. Instead, he fearfully makes his way to the Highway Bridge. Convinced a life at sea and in Gloucester will bring nothing but misery, the man begins to cross.

Now check *this* out:

Each step he takes in knee-high waders becomes heavier and heavier. Yet the old man trudges on. He arrives at the base of the Bridge under low-laying fog. He can see the mainland. But the gravity of Gloucester won't let him move. He strains forward with all his might, muscles aching, trying to slash through the chilling nor'east wind. *Niente.* It's as though the island is a magnet, a vacuum, pulling the ambition from the poor fisherman's soul. In agony, he drops to his knees, thrashing the frozen ground before him.

And then there was this sound.

It did not come from the man.

It came from the wind. A wind that blew right through the Bridge. A wind that split the night.

That wind said something to the broken fisherman and dragged him back to Gloucester with purpose. The wind said this: "Fire Insurance."

A new way of life was born. The old man retired comfortably to Cocaine Lane.

•

There are subtle and not so subtle ways for someone in the neighborhood to flaunt his or her newfound wealth. Pimps drive prettier Cadillacs. Material girls have their cheekbones raised above their eyebrows. Here, we have slumlords.

That Bridge and that wind was there for that old man like Section 8 housing was there for Goita. She was able to buy decrepit apartment buildings in Gloucester's historic West End with money kept tucked under a mattress for safe keeping. (Many Italian and Portuguese immigrants still stow cash in this manner, having lost trust in the constantly failing bank businesses of their native countries.) In time, Goita began to charge exorbitant fees to her own relatives living in her apartments. Soon, one building became two and two became four. How? Because Goita's relatives kept multiplying. Still do.

And that, friends and neighbors, is what slumlording's all about.

Though Goita's and Johnny's families are bottled in the West End, Johnny's buddies live in the far reaches of town. (This can be quite inconvenient if you're too young to own a driver's license, unless you don't mind the hour and a half ride from Lexington Avenue in Magnolia to Thatcher Road in Rockport on a CATA bus.)

For example, Vito Ditalini's family resides in the ghost-village of Magnolia, Gloucester's southernmost section. Magnolia is considered a village because it doesn't have a gas station, bank, traffic light or breakfast nook. Most of Gloucester's residents don't consider Magnolia part of Gloucester because it lies on the other side of the Cut, entirely mainland, bordering Manchester-by-the-Sea. But most of Gloucester's residents are happy Magnolia exists, since residents there pay the most taxes of any section of the city.

What does one get for paying such hefty tariffs, besides an occupied firehouse every other year? Not much. But Magnolia residents like the Ditalinis recently got a huge boost from local politicians discussing how to use the mass of cleared acreage that used to maintain the city landfill. For decades the city settled on unlawfully dumping chemicals there. But nowadays, remarkably, there's a new tradition of flattening and seeding dirty swamplands and toxic dumping grounds in Magnolia to construct massive soccer fields. In fact, the whole village thrives on the youth soccer industry. Yes, if there's land to be used in Magnolia, it's used for one of two things: Soccer fields or shitty condos.

Residents there often stage round-the-clock soccer marathons, running naked and waving banners about town. Mailmen deliver packages delicately balanced on their heads. Vito and his girlfriend sleep in cleats, and they're not the only ones. The Ditalinis own and operate a giant conveyor belt that relays quartered orange slices to spent players and soccer enthusiasts. Vito even has an aunt who styled her hair after a famous soccer star. She looks like someone shot a sick otter off her forehead.

Outsiders may view Magnolians as oddballs: Soccer-yearning hooligans dancing and playing on hazardous landfills. But as any Magnolian worth his or her salt will tell you: When you see three-legged strikers and five-armed goalkeepers dominating the 2028 Beijing Olympics, you'll know where they came from.

•

Think Magnolia is weird? Try this:

For years, Sal Rigatoni's family catered to the plumbing and heating needs of fruit loops inhabiting Dogtown Common, an intensely wooded area rumored to attract derelicts and witchcrafters long ago. Today, the nuttiest people in Gloucester reside in the northernmost section of the city. It's where the Rigatoni's moved to follow business. It's called Lanesville. Lanesville is Gloucester's version of Area 51. Here's a typical conversation overheard in Lanesville on any given day:

Pagan:	What time is the exorcism?
Ghoul:	Sundown, my liege.
Alien:	Won't that interfere with the Dance of Fire after the pig roast?
Carolers:	We sacrificed the pig already?
Oinks the Pig:	Shit—Taxi!

•

Still, one must go to the center of Gloucester to find a strong pulse. That's where the bars and boats are. And that's what Goita's buildings are built around.

Goita's buildings have similar distinguishing features: faded white paint and rusty gutters; three-story decks constructed without legal permits; wide, old-fashioned exterior asbestos paneling. All are chock-full of Cuzzins. None have a yard worth mowing.

The decks are invaluable to occupants. In Johnny Ziti's situation, the deck works like a display case. Cuzzins swagger onto decktops shirtless, trying to gain the attention of passerby. Simple tasks like screwing a lightbulb or carrying a full cooler often requires the noticeably painful flexing of every muscle in a Cuzzin's body. The larger the audience, the more strenuous flexing becomes. But it's after everyday chores are completed that real showmanship begins. Though naturally enough, older, larger-muscled men make their way to the front of the display case, the key for all participants is comfortability. There's a secret to being cool, and even though most Cuzzins don't know it, it doesn't stop them from trying.

The tip?

Be completely and thoroughly preoccupied with absolutely nothing at all.

An experienced Cuz may reveal his expertise by giving a concerned look at a choppy waterfront, or a knowing chuckle after clueless SUV drivers try U-turning in front of the Statue, something a native would *never* do. Plus, available ladies find thinking Cuzzes irresistible. A sure-fire trick is to loudly predict when the Cut will open for boats to pass through the canal. In such instances, speed and timing are crucial.

One time, a hopeful Cuz-to-be, probably a high school senior, announced the Cut would soon open, noting the long line of whale watch boats bobbing in Gloucester Harbor. Unfortunately, the Cut was already gaping, the Boulevard compounded with lines of traffic. And don't think for a second the other Cuzzins let him get off easy. The scent of blood is strong on these decks, and such errors are open invitations to cries of "Loozah!" and several unannounced charleyhorses.

•

Adolescent dating in Gloucester is a humbling and at times humiliating affair. Such was the case for Johnny and his Cuzzins as they cannonballed into puberty. Bursting hormones infect this city's youth as early as fourth or fifth grade. For most, this is when the flirtatious part of the mating process begins. Smitten girls looking to attract a young boy's attention may strike him with repeated blows to the stomach during recess, while curious and confused boys wrestle and drool on one another through dental headgear. Those who find they are not attracted to the opposite sex find solace in dressing in black and listening to mopey, turtleneck-wearing limeys in lipstick on college radio stations.

Some children raised in stricter religious families have their naughty parts stowed away until marriage, a fraction of which are arranged. Yes, these people are fucked in the noodle. Let's move on.

As children age, flirting becomes more involved. Crushes are revealed with classroom whispers and secret notes passed about. In time, handholding and shy locker-talk shapes into dating. A quality date for a Gloucester preteen couple would be spending time at a Little League game at Boudreau Field, walking over the giant hill behind the outfield fence toward Cressy Beach, and enjoying an ice cream or motor oil-dipped onion rings at the Cupboard.

When kids sift into O'Maley Junior High School, their bodies begin to warp, contort, explode and blossom. The body grows fast. There's little room for experimenting. Little girls grow into Glochicks, carrying fashionable purses filled with cheap cigarettes and tube socks for stuffing bras. Boys reach these years pathetically, believing peach fuzz above their top lip, the same fuzz that covers their asses, passes for mustaches. They also discover back acne and have hardons like candlepins.

Sure, there are a couple school-sponsored dances around town, where you pound beers in the parking lot, try shaking your ass, and come to terms for the first time with your blinding whiteness. But don't be mistaken. These kids know that's just child's play.

Seasoned and savvy as they enter young adulthood, the high school years are equally eventful. The prettiest young women start dating unemployed twenty-somethings. Guys are busy screwing bedspreads in preparation for March Madness, a game of sexual mischief based somewhat on the famous national college basketball tournament. The entire month is devoted to an all-out rush to see who can get the most girls. Points are tallied through an intricate scoring system. Good score: Sleeping with a senior cheerleader or gymnast in her dad's Volkswagen. Bad score: A flapjack-sized hickey from a freshman with cleft lip and lazyfoot. It takes a mighty special Cuz to last the full four-plus weeks. The game usually lasts three days.

Growing up ain't easy for anyone. Not even the Johnny Zitis of the world. Case in point: The implosion of 4EVA, the Gloucester boy-band Johnny fronted throughout puberty.

You see, before 'NSYNC and the Backstreet Boys, even before New Kids on the Block, there was a group of idiotic white boys from Gloucester who had all the makings of superstardom. They were awesome—*wigged* awesome. And they were *totally Glosta!* 4EVA was a phenomenon. There were four members: Totebag, D.L.S.H., Headgear, and Johnny Ziti. Totebag was the bookish one. He carried Judy Blume and Encyclopedia Brown wherever he went. D.L.S.H. was the only known entertainer with four initials to his name. He thought D.L.S.H. was short for Delicious. (The others kept him away from the money.) Headgear was the quiet one. He didn't sing the entire time 4EVA was together. But he had a mouth wrapped in steel—and chicks dig steel. Well, 12-year old chicks do. Then there was Johnny—the misunderstood kid from the wrong side of jungle gym. He was street tough. In every 4EVA photo shoot, Johnny posed on the moped.

They made their own costumes and did their own choreography. Like all bands whose fans still watch Nickelodeon,

ST. PETER'S FIASCO 51

they needed the perfect look. And damn, did 4EVA ever look the part.

Before their first gig, they all scrawled the New Coke logo into their crewcuts. It made them stronger. Instead of gaudy jewelry and medallions, they dangled hubcaps and fishbowls from their necks, (for a short time Johnny just lugged Headgear's baby brother over his shoulder from show to show), before finally settling on their trademark trashcan lids.

True Gloucester boys to the core, they all dated high school seniors named Jen who spent way too much time at the sun parlor. Embittered and gin-soaked session musicians wrote songs for them like "Yeah Baby Yeah", "Love Baby Love", and "Baby Love Yeah." And before you knew it, they began to tour everywhere (Thank you, CATA).

Unfortunately, being a teen pop star isn't all wine and roses. Or in 4EVA's case, fruit juice and Aqua Net. There was friction in the band. Totebag never rebounded after whispers of his seedy personality began to surface. He was rumored to have gone home with anyone who donated 20 or more dollars to PBS. Then, poor Headgear's crooked teeth eventually only required an overnight retainer—he struggled with his identity. They had to get rid of D.L.S.H. because he couldn't get his initials straight. One day he'd feel Delicious, the next he felt F.I.N.E. The day he was canned, 4EVA's manager asked D.L.S.H. how he felt. All he said was "I.M.O.K." That's difficult.

To make matters worse, Johnny became violently dependent on Silly String. First he sprayed it, then ate it, and that led to snorting. Message to future Menudo members: When your manager barges into a dank motel room to find you despondent and covered in hot pink foam—you know there's a problem.

Then, in the middle of what would be 4EVA's last show, The Artist Formerly Known as Headgear went crazy. They were in the middle of "Love Baby Love"—no wait—it was "Yeah Baby Yeah"—when the pressure of losing his identity finally got to him. In a fit of rage, he bit the head off a chocolate Easter bunny.

The audience at the retirement home that Sunday morning sat stunned and appalled, then slowly dozed off.

Word spread fast. There were protests and picket lines all over Cape Ann. Some said they were protesting Reverend Moon and the Moonies (another popular band at the time), but Johnny swears it was the chocolate bunny people. It was the first time 4EVA's integrity was questioned. They were forced into permanent hiatus.

Giving up chocolate bunnies was the toughest decision Headgear made—tougher than disbanding 4EVA. But it has made him the honest professional lamppost scratcher he is today.

As for Johnny, he thought they would last through high school—or 4EVA—whichever came first. Seeing how they prefigured all these fabricated, prepubescent con artists years later, he just wished he took the time to smell the roses. Sadly, with six fluid ounces of hot pink Silly String in his nose, Johnny never got the chance.

Oh, the humanity.

We now return you to the present.

•

With little time to spare before sundown, Tina Cafeena decides a proper apology to Johnny is in order. She asks if he wants to go for a quick ride around the Back Shore, which can mean only one thing: awkward sex while parked in front of Niles Beach. Unfortunately, Rigga invites himself for the ride, thinking they're going to "spahk up the sweet leafs." Johnny doesn't object. Johnny ain't too bright. In fact, he's about the same shade as Rigga.

Niles Beach is narrow. Its parking lot lies parallel to the road leading to an historic lighthouse at the tip of Eastern Point. Tourists visit the lighthouse as well as the quaint Beauport Museum, despite a wobbly security guard employed by residents of the private road to pick his fingernails in front of the stone pillars. A manmade breakwater constructed ages ago shoots off rocks the lighthouse sits atop, providing safe harbor during inclement weather. Abenaki Indians once inhabited the area around Eastern Point when the first weird, white, religiously slanted riffraff migrated from Europe. The Indians and marauders enjoyed a fruitful, healthy relationship (according to weird, white, religiously slanted textbooks). Why today, a resident of Eastern Point would gladly allow an Abenaki to vacuum the Yacht Club after a champagne clambake.

As it happens, Tina Cafeena pulls her Plymouth into one of the parking slots young lovers of the city have made famous. Rigga jumps out and joins the security guard for a round of vodkas drunk out of Budweiser cans, leaving his friends to recklessly contaminate the hatchback with DNA. Johnny looks over his sweetheart.

I've been to the otha side of the Bridge and back now, he says. I hafta go.

Why now? she asks. What about Fiesta?

Oh T . . . We'll be back. Think I'd miss Fiesta? It's just a hahmless trip.

Then why go? What's so special on *that* side of the Bridge?

Trust me T . . . My god, it's like magic . . . You don't know 'til you've done it. Go down the otha side, pass Nichols candies . . . the old drive-in . . . then you're outta Glosta . . . past Manchesta and Essex—I mean way past . . . then Bevalee—and there's this Burga King there T, next to a gas station . . . you wouldn't believe it T . . . right off the highway . . . and they're *always hiring* . . . Then the malls: First Liberty Tree, then North Shore . . . After that—the road opens up—*four lanes!* Traffic gets wiggid heavy . . . Then, afta a while T—you see it.

See what?

Boston. The Tobin Bridge. It's like this gate to heaven or suntin'. You see it and you *gotta* go ova it! It's not like the bridges here!

I know you gotta go then. I just wish it wasn't now.

T—if I don't go now—I may never go. There might be suntin' for us ova there babe! Did I tell you there's a Burga King *right off* the highway? *Right* off!

Aw Johnny. Just shuddup and love me!

Please don't make me explain what happens next. Let's just close our eyes for a paragraph and let the pain pass . . .

•

After the deed is done, and sweet Jesus-Allah-Buddha does it get done, the three head for Rigga's parents' place to stock up for the festivities. From the cellar they gather another cooler, two gallons of Aqua Net, four sixteen-ounce tubes of zinc to coat their skin, teeth whitener, and whatever else they think those at the apartment might have forgotten.

Tina transports the Cuzzins to Goita's building, and more importantly, to the hot rod. In no time, Johnny and Rigga are petting and coddling the IROC. For a moment, Tina notices an ex-girlfriend of Johnny's across the street. They exchange piercing glares. Johnny's body may be up for grabs. There could be a concession or a catfight. Either way, Johnny will be standing just a few feet away, squeaky freakin' clean.

At once, Tina Cafeena's mosquito-like attention span is drawn to a heated confrontation between the guys at the IROC. Tony Baloney's announced tonight is too important for him *not* to drive to Boston, so *he'll* be behind the wheel. The argument however, is not about who's driving. It's about who sits shotgun, thereby becoming Tony's right-hand man. Expectedly, Johnny and Rigga go toe to toe. Gold chains tangle, and they are kept from chucking knuckles only when other Cuzzins leap over the deck railings . . . shirtless.

The two eventually reconcile by masculinely hugging without

touching. Lumbering across the street is Petey Meatballeyes, another longtoothed Glosta legend and Tony's lifelong sidekick. He smacks Johnny and Rigga on their bony shoulders. "Tony says I'm in," Meatballeyes declares. "So you fuggin' guys can fugeddabout shotgun."

3

And Now a Word from Our Sponsor

In 1985, Chevrolet Camaro introduced the IROC-Z. It was the offshoot of 1982's third generation Camaros: the Berlinetta, Sports Coupe and Z28. The new IROC-Z came with aluminum wheels, Goodyear Gatorback tires, fog lamps, "CAMARO" on the front license plate panel, body-colored valances, Delco-Bilstein rear gas shocks, special front struts, increased spring rates, special jounce bumpers, five degrees of caster in front wheel alignment, "wonderbar" front frame rail stiffener, special valving in steering for increased steering effort, larger rear stabilizer bar with stiffer bushings, IROC-Z exterior decals and interior dash badge, and a thinner two-color lower body stripe.

In later models, the 85mph speedometer was replaced with a new 145mph unit, along with a new coat/base coat paint. They also had an externally mounted third brake light on the hatch glass.

In 1987 Camaro's original plant in Norwood, Ohio ceased producing Camaros. This would spell doom for IROC lovers. Less and less IROCs were produced the following years. The Chevrolet IROC contract was eventually terminated. No IROC-Z's were produced after December 31, 1989. All that remained were IROC-Z convertibles and late model 1LE's.

Yup, that's what the brochure says.

•

Didn't really need to know that, didja?

•

The IROC-Z is the main attraction on Stacy Boulevard. Tony Baloney and Sal Rigatoni quit jobs slinging pizzas and pounding nails to spend more time cruising. The only other vehicle on the streets that could possibly pose a challenge is the giant black Bigfoot three-quarter ton truck driven by Gloucester High Vocational School graduate Lorenzo Pimento. Not only is Lorenzo literally head and shoulders above the crowd, but the kid can shake a stick shift. Fiesta after Fiesta, he piles more underage girls in his truck than anyone on either side of the Bridge. Both the *IROC-Z* and the Bigfoot *America* draw so many ladies, when they roam Western Avenue, hardly a peep is heard from nearby and predominately female Endicott College.

So far, Johnny's feeling uneasy about passing up the Boulevard and departing from home so close to Fiesta. There's been pretty potent cat tranquilizers batted around the North Shore lately, and a crowded backseat could lead to sweaty headlocks, the last thing Tony wants in his car.

It's pushing nine o'clock now, and may be too late to doubleback for last call in Gloucester. Tony's trying to get everybody on the same page. Johnny's finally changing out of his stained shirt. Vito's getting an earful from his girlfriend for forgetting to buy frozen mudslide mix. Rigga just wants to see a pair of tits. As if that weren't enough, Yo-Yo OneNut, an old-school Portagee who usually mans the back of the *IROC-Z*, suddenly opts to watch the Air Guitar competition at Old Timer's. At the last second, Yo-Yo decides to hang out with Joe Tomatoes, a young man who will never drive ten minutes on Route 128 for anything. Tomatoes convinced Yo-Yo that Air Guitar Night wouldn't suck and the Wet T-shirt Contest may feature someone with nipples above her bellybutton.

Tony Baloney's *not* happy.

Tony:	What's this about you backin' out Yo?
Yo-Yo:	Nah Tone, it's nothin' like that. It's just, y'know, Fiesta.
Tony:	Fiesta?
Joe Tomatoes:	Yeah Tone, any otha time and we'd be there.
Tony:	Who said anything about you, Cuz? You been eating retahd soup for lunch?
Yo-Yo:	He's just saying Tone, y'know, Boston's a long ways away. And it's Fiesta, Cuz. How come you're leavin' now?
Tony:	How come? Haven't I taught you anything Cuz? I chase chicks. It's who I am. It's what I do. And I don't care if it's Fiesta or Christmas fuggin' mornin'. When I feel like a Keepah, I *feel like a Keepah*. Awright?
Joe Tomatoes:	Cuz, he's just sayin'—
Tony:	Let me tell you somethin' Joe. You're a good kid. I played hoops with your brotha. Known him a long time. But you got a long way to go before you get in a cah like this. Got it, Cuz?
Yo-Yo:	Hey Tone, tell ya what. Afta Fiesta Sunday I'll hit Boston with ya, okay? No questions asked. Alright Cuz?
Tony:	Yah sure, we'll break bread like real fuggin' gangstas. Now run along with ya little boyfriend there Cuz . . . My cah's full anyway.

•

Guys get funny feelings about who may or may not be in local bars on a particular night. They know they'll see the same people. They know 75% of the crowd will be guys just like them. *But you never know.* Maybe it's some Rockport girl's twenty-first birthday. She couldn't possibly celebrate in archaic Rockport. Rockport's a dry town. (Their motto: Come to Rockport, fossilize, and argue over property lines and 18th century statutes. Good day.) So maybe she's in downtown Gloucester, full of B-52's, feeling the walls down Main Street. *You never know.* It's what keeps Cuzzins coming back.

There certainly are times when the chicky fishing's good. Thanksgiving weekend is the first weekend college freshmen return home. The night before the holiday everyone goes to Pratty's, a bar near the waterfront, and stands shoulder to shoulder with folks who graduated years before them and those who haven't graduated yet. It's a killer opportunity to see where you've come from and what you will become. The holiday itself is reserved for the big annual football game against Danvers High. The rest of the weekend is a blur.

Perhaps the most interesting time for prosperity is Memorial Day Weekend. It's the first weekend everyone is home from school and back on beaches and in bars. It's also the most opportune time to evaluate the summer's crop of 21-year-olds.

We're pretty big on tradition here.

•

Vibes *do* play an important role in gauging nighttime activities. Joe Tomatoes felt his friend Yo-Yo wasn't ready for prime time, and wheedled him to stay. Years ago, a coolerman with a history of creepy premonitions named Louie Roma was aboard the Beverly-bound 1977 Mustang *Victory*. After dozing off at Exit 17, Roma awoke screaming, demanding they immediately pull into the breakdown lane. "I saw it again," Roma cried. *Victory* shotgunner Nino Bruschetti was the only crewman tolerant enough to listen. He reluctantly asks Roma about his vision.

I'm lyin' on the beach, Roma explains, next to the most beautiful woman I've seen. The mornin' sun is soft and warm. She smiles at me. We are, like, so in love. We can't stop lookin' at each otha. It's like she penetrated the chickenwya around my heart. But there's somethin' wrong. She does somethin', I don't know, curls her eyebrow or squints a certain way—that's so familiar. Then, it hits me. *'Do you know the Orlandos on Summer Street?'*

Yes, she says.

And the Palazollas on Marina Drive?

Yes.

And the Granite Street Asaros?

Yes.

And what about the Sanfillipos at the Fort?

You mean the ones next to the Aiellos? she says.

No, I say, the ones between the Testaverdes and the Scolas.

Of course I do, she says. Then she gets this look on her face. *Wait a minute, she says. How do you know them? Tell me! How do you know all them?*

I can't stand the pain. *They're my cousins, I say. They're all my first cousins. Why?* And looking at her then I believe I was looking at a clubbed haddock.

Because, she whispers, they're my first cousins too. Louie Roma collapsed into Bruschetti's arms, looking at him through bleary, beaten eyes. *She's family, Nino . . .*

The *Victory* crew wordlessly turned 'round for the Bridge.

Too ridiculous? Check out the wedding announcements in the local paper sometime. It's frightening. Talk about keeping it in the family . . .

•

With OneNut off hooting at droopy women and middle-aged men singing *My Sharona*, Tony Baloney invites Meatballeyes to join the crew. Meatballeyes achieved minor legendary status last summer when he fought a hoops player from Beverly and stole his girl. Back in the day, he was a three-sport standout at the Factory. He's also been known to spring for bachelor party strippers. In other words, Meatballeyes is solid.

When Meatballeyes hears Tony's leaving, he jets across the street to Johnny's apartment, where the "shotgun" argument is taking place. "Rookies," he thinks.

When IROC's leave Gloucester, brimming with Cuzzins, they do so with trunks loaded with the highest regarded personal maintenance equipment money can buy. Cuzzins can last a week in the most obnoxious Euro-dance clubs in Boston.

Johnny and Rigga fill the back with toiletries. Tony and Meatballeyes are the most prepared. They have suit jackets, slacks, khakis, jeans, satin shirts, extra boxers, silk boxers, hard combs, toothpicks, leather-banded watches, flashy rings, clip-on nose and eyebrow rings, (depending on which club they arrive at), alligator-skin shoes, ball caps, a carton of squids, handfuls of narcotics, beer, ATM cards, zit cream, baby oil, and plenty of towels for beach-crashing.

The list may seem staggering, but Cuzzins know how to make due. The *IROC-Z* has precious little available space, a compact glove compartment, pouches behind the front seats, five excitable passengers, and of course, a hand-washed carpet floor. Not an inch of space is wasted before the crew feels fully equipped.

The cooler and clothing are the most valuable items for after-hours. Gloucester bars and liquor stores close ridiculously early and big city-dwelling girls who may come home in the *IROC-Z* may not expect the fifteen-degree difference in temperature between Boston and Gloucester. (Lorenzo Pimento smartly leaves a pup tent in his Bigfoot for such occasions.) There are many ways to lure unsure company "up the line" to Cape Ann.

Leaving the island is a mighty culture shock for the uninitiated. As attitudes and styles change with times, so too, do females. To put it bluntly, you just won't find honest, Roman-Catholic Glosta girls go-go dancing in thongs and pasties around Boston's old Combat Zone. When Cuzzins navigate and network the dance floor, they align themselves with an amazing array of different women.

The following is one Cuzzin's scouting report on Boston's

dating scene, translated here from Cuz to improper American (Odds on consummating meaningful relationship supplied by Three Miles Out Offshore Betting):

1. **Schoolies.** Slang for students and nannies. It's no secret. They're everywhere. As the saying goes, "They're young, fun, and full of . . ." Well, you know. Boston, known as the Athens of the West, is home to dozens of places for higher learning. (Has anyone seen Athens lately?) Each autumn brings thousands of newcomers to the Hub, most notably a steady stream of dickheads and almost-Yentas from Long Island. Problem is, those numbers make flirting too easy for Cuzzins. Anyone with a rod and reel can fish for Schoolies. Real men wrassle gators. (Odds: 2 to 1)
2. **Medheads.** ATF Canine Units can't sniff drugs like these pros. The Unsober know their junk. And if they know their junk, they know Gloucester. They're not interested in romance, just spacing out. A nice, long drive along the Cape Ann coastline, away from the noise and confusion of a hopping-mad cityscape, always does the trick for these fallen angels. Cuzzes try to avoid them unless their stash is desperately low, especially if the girls look like they've been left in the rain a few days. (Odds: 50 to 1)
3. **Chicks with Picks.** Ah, musicians. Always a mixed bag. You can hit the jackpot, say an uninhibited flutist with a black belt in Oral. Or, you could end up with crabs and a pile of demo tapes. Enter with extreme caution. (Odds: 300 to 1)
4. **Barracudas.** Jet setters. Usually from Europe and the Middle East. These ladies take private flights from Lisbon or London or Dubai, stand in front of ritzy establishments with baby seal handbags and spotted owl nail polish, just so they can be seen holding $300 glasses of wine for a *few hours*! Then they keep flying west towards L.A. to outrace curfews! (Odds: no line) (Odds on author praying for World War III: real, *real* good.)

5. **Keepahs.** The Loch Ness of Ladies. Keepahs are classy, well-educated, professional women. But they ain't sugar and spice and everything nice. Why? *Attitude.* Keepahs have chewed and spit every type of potential suitor possible: smalltown football heroes, yuppies, hollow-headed lunatics from rich families who get $10,000 gifts just for graduating fucking prep school, you name it. They've been known to ruin naive frat brothers with one steely glare.

Keepahs know how to spend money, especially when it isn't their own. They can pry a workingman's paycheck before the two could share a kiss. Cuzzes are drawn to high-maintenance women, which covers most of Boston. And let's face it, Cuzzes are basically high-maintenance women with penises. They read the same magazines, speak the same language, and put equally absurd amounts of time into their appearance. But Keepahs think Cuzzes are beneath them. A Newbury Street makeover trumps a Cuz every time. To avoid such boorish confrontations, the savviest Keepahs congregate at upscale bars and restaurants where professional athletes and businessmen frequent. Some have a specific man in mind, right down to knowing his batting average. Others simply go for anything in a Porsche.

Quoting directly from my source now: "These fuggin' women, all they want is sophistication. Hey, sorry ladies. I ain't no Chuck fuggin' Norris." (Odds: Ever hear the one about the monosyllabic idiot who marries into beauty, intellect and wealth, becomes a respected member of his community, and lives happily ever after? Me neither.)

•

Incidentally, a familiar "pahk and spahk" point in Gloucester is the end of Commercial Street, where the wharf begins or ends, depending where you're coming from. The road rolls right towards the Atlantic, stopping at Producers Fish Company, a one-time famous fish dealing market now gutted by fire. Producers used to haul fresh fish from boats onto their dock, ice the fish, and store it in huge walk-in freezers for supermarket chains or whatnot to transport.

The 10,000 square foot lot abuts the ocean and offers an exquisite harbor vista. It's conveniently located in the lovely West End section of the city, just a short walk from the downtown business district, area beaches and train station. A spacious yet private parking area on this dead-end road provides ample room for several vehicles. Below the lot rests an opulent oil tank, still in perfect working condition. This land is immediately available. Interested parties are asked to submit serious bids with PFC's president. Better yet, contact the president's first-born. Damnit, they're just good people.

•

Such useless information is the nesting-stuff of Gloucester folk life.

4

Off of the Island and Into the Streets

The crew is ready for departure. Everything's packed, all precious fuels and fluids are full, everybody has cash, and the beer is icy. All that's left is figuring the seating arrangement. Johnny and Rigga, the others feel, should be separated on account of their "shotgun" dispute. Tina Cafeena seizes the chance to drag Johnny back into the apartment for a review of their set rules: No talking to other girls, no driving back shitfaced, a phone call immediately upon returning, blah, blah, blah. As far as Johnny's concerned, everything Tina says goes in one ear and out the other.

The two nudge and paw one another on Johnny's futon. Outside, the *IROC-Z* engine hums. Johnny can't see the car, but feels a rush of burnt rubber course through his body. Humidity creeps through the screen door. "Fog's probably rollin' ova the Bridge," says Tina. "Betta be careful." There's a shout from outside. It's Meatballeyes. His gel's getting cold, it's time to roll.

Without a moment to spare, Johnny steals away to the bathroom. After sealing the door, he privately thumbs his buttonfly open. There resting comfortably is Meester Joe, slumped like a slug on Johnny's underbelly. Johnny keeps a hushed voice.

Meester Joe? This is it! We're goin' to Boston! We're gonna get Keepahs! Just like I promised.

You make Meester Joe happy. Meester Joe's waited veddy long time for this.

I know Meester Joe. Are you as excited as I am?

Give me a second Johnny. Don't outthink yourself now gringo. Even black bears stray from honey a few days after hibernation.

Oh. Right! Okay—here we go!

•

The air is filled with anxiety down in the driveway. Tony just ran from his parole officer, Vito's transferring bags of booze into his young girlfriend's car, and Goita's yapping about the loitering kids. "The cops'll clear you out and my house will be mahked!" she hollers. And then there's this journey over the Bridge so close to Fiesta. Returning for 12:30 a.m. closing time looks more and more like an impossibility. Northbound traffic will be a mess.

A few stragglers try convincing Tony's guys that where they *should* be is downtown. There are definitely reservations amongst the crew, but the boys need to get laid. Any other time, and it's beers and stiff drinks at Cameron's. But not tonight, especially when Tony's gone through the trouble of tidying his car for the trip. It is after all, an IROC on its way to Boston. Refusing to go could result in long-term Boulevard banishment. And one thing about Gloucester's Cuzzes: a promise made is a promise kept.

Tony calls for one last round of shots. All agree on tequila. Tina Cafeena's not one for shots, and her stomach starts to burn. Meatballeyes hands her the last couple ounces of his beer to chase the taste. The lights of the Vegas-like altar used during Fiesta blinks in strings.

Five men leaving the island on the eve of St. Peter's Fiesta is a bold and ballsy move. Goita marches around the lot telling the others they are not welcome around her building while Johnny is gone. She makes sure Tina has the only set of extra keys. Johnny asks his landlord if she'd like to hold his hand while he pees. She threatens to call Tony's officer.

"Just kidding sir," says Johnny.

The Cuzzins board the Camaro. Tony Baloney's driving. Petey Meatballeyes is riding shotgun. Johnny's behind Tony and Rigga's behind Petey, with coolerman Vito in the middle as a buffer. The *IROC-Z* is leaving Gloucester.

The car purrs onto Western Ave., nearing the Cut. Tony flicks on the right directional. "You betta fuggin' call!" screeches Tina. "Quit flappin'!" Johnny yells back. Tony blares the horn. The crew goes wild. Petey flings a bottle out the window as the *IROC-Z* screams past the Factory over the steep hill of Centennial Ave. At the end of Centennial they'll turn left onto Washington Street, heading straight for the rotary. From there, the big hunching Bridge is in sight.

As soon as they pull out of the driveway, beers are fed to every crewman. Vito, sitting on the middle hump of the backseat, controls the cooler. He gets first choice of beer for having the crappy seat. The Cuzzins compare girlfriends to past girlfriends, paychecks and promotions. All can explain what a kitty-corner is, or the virtues of oil-based paint, or how point spreads are determined. All can explain how each Cuz is related to the other: It's family that keeps them from leaving Gloucester. Leave the house unmarried and you're a pariah. Leave it and have a kid and you're out of the will. Leave it and have a kid with someone from outside town and you can kiss your blood roots goodbye. Nevertheless, the more exposure one has off the island, the greater the chance of someday leaving for good becomes. Understandably, so much talking and thinking leads to serious drinking. Cold, bottled beers are first to go. Then cold cans. By the end of the journey, a Cuz could be scraping for warm Narragansetts.

•

St. Peter is the patron saint of fishermen. The Fiesta is the weeklong annual Italian fishing festival. The majority of revelers forego the days of solemn prayers and focus on the four-day carnival at the Fort in Gloucester's West End, lasting from Thursday through Sunday. It is during the carnival that fireworks, parades and sporting events take place.

Before the carnival became part of the celebration, there was the novena, a processional prayer service for fishing families asking for peaceful weather and abundant catches. Everyone in the community kept their doors unlocked and feasted on homemade dishes and wine. In time, fishermen began competing in seine boat races and Greasy Pole contests.

Ornate, elaborate altars were constructed at the Fort to rest a statue of Saint Peter. When statue bearers lead a candlelight procession from the Shrine at St. Peter's Club to the Fiesta Altar, the festival begins.

Meanwhile, thousands gather as music, entertainment and children's games fill the weekend. The Fiesta only slows to accommodate the races, the Greasy Pole, and the Blessing of the Fleet by the Archbishop of Boston (unless, of course, he's busy giving his deposition).

On Sunday, after trophies for the weekend's winners are awarded, after a giant fireworks display has ceased, the statue of St. Peter is returned to the Shrine under a hail of confetti and song.

Of all events, the most highly anticipated is the Greasy Pole contest. The premise is to walk a forty-foot axle-greased telephone pole protruding from a wooden platform five yards or so above the surface of Gloucester Harbor, and capture a flag nailed to its end. Contestants are usually fishermen or a fisherman's family member participating under a relative's name.

It is an honor to be asked to walk.

The rules have been tinkered with over the years. Until recently, Saturdays were the preliminaries. Saturday's winner earns the right to walk Sunday, which remains strictly reserved for past champions. Today, people have a chance to walk Friday to get to Saturday.

Anyhow, once walkers arrive at the platform, veteran contestants step the pole first. Etiquette is easy to follow: No one grabs the flag during the first courtesy go around. (Violators are flogged beachside.) And, make sure the guy walking before you doesn't drown.

When someone snatches the flag and smacks the water, the other walkers skitter off the pole and usher the victor to Pavilion Beach towards the Altar. As the winner is carried away on the other contestants' shoulders, random cries of, *"Tutti muti?"* ("Whya you no speaka?") are answered by the surrounding mob's, *"Viva San Pi-e-e-etro!"*

This gives everyone involved a chance to pretend they're Catholic.

The names of the champions quickly become part of Fiesta lore.

Folks, I am not makin' this shit up. Come visit sometime, drop off your nieces, then leave.

5

The Scrotum Pole

Some outbound Camaros from Gloucester still cruise Beverly and Salem, few get all the way to Boston. It's further from the island but the center of attraction. It can take under 45 minutes to reach Boston in heavy traffic in a late model IROC. Route 128 trickles south-southwest towards the Hub into I-95, some 35-40 miles from Gloucester. Like Beverly and Salem, Boston's teeming population offers sights normally unseen to Gloucester natives, like natural blondes. The clubs are crazier, the dancing more frenzied. The nights start later and last longer. The hunters and the hunted always find their way to the capital.

Trips take place between Thursdays and Saturdays. In rare instances, momentum after a day of beer softball may warrant a Sunday excursion. When home, any day of the week can be a party day. Between O'Maley and the high school, everyone from town has had more than their fair share of housebound Fridays and Saturdays. This is why road trips are so cherished.

Boozing and cooing aren't all these pilgrimages are about. Fast food, sweat, and cologne, like road salt on the exterior, take its toll on vehicles. This requires constant care. The backseat crew is responsible for empties and wrappers, crumbs and spills. Nobody wants to be seen in the parking lot checking for grease spots on vests or scrounging cans from under seats, so on-the-road partying is constantly monitored and somewhat controlled. If Cuzzins travel through burbs like Manchester-by-the-Sea, they must be alert to police cars set 15 yards apart for speed traps and sobriety checks. Cuzzins floss, divide breath mints and scan the radio. Some shotgunners automatically dial through to the region's foremost techno stations without thinking.

Everyone's job on the crew is well understood. The driver is captain, and it's his duty to show off the car, meaning lots of time barreling through the passing lane. Shotgunner is nearly important. He must adjust heating and air conditioning so armpits won't sweat excessively or gelled hair go limp, as well as manage the stereo. As mentioned before, the cooler's always in the heart of the vehicle. Those seated by rear windows must look for parking spaces, bands of drunken girls stumbling down sidewalks, and cop cars. Staring and head-swiveling never becomes a bore—college girls who can't hold their liquor are everywhere.

•

Tony Baloney's driven to Boston dozens of times. He's also gone to New York City, Cape Cod, Providence and Montreal. He grew up near the junkyard by the railroad tracks and had a kid not long after acquiring his license. When he wasn't driving a tow truck or watching wrestling, Tony took classes at North Shore Community College and earned an English degree. That is, he read four books on gay socialist poetry, the older stuff. He got a job at an auto parts store at the insistence of his child's mother, allowing him to combine car know-how with his college degree. "Ya not ignurint," she would say. "Yuh wickit fu'in smaht."

In no time, Tony could recognize any model car, truck or van. And the connections he made at work reaped great deals on used cars and parts. His first car was a Pontiac Trans Am, and with the Trans Am came Tony's first nights on the Boulevard. When the Trans Am fell out of fashion, he bought a jeep. Although the gas mileage isn't good and maintenance a ballbreaker, topless jeeps allow everyone in the neighborhood to see who is riding in it and hear what they're listening to. Tony became glued to the Boulevard. He smoked dope with his mother's new boyfriend, Bobby Zucci, at a family cottage in New Hampshire for a couple summers, but the Boulevard remained home.

Tony's mother, Tulip, and her boyfriend Bobby would leave the cottage every June for the Fiesta. It also gave them a chance to keep tabs on Tony. Bobby and Tony had similar fascinations with cars, and when Bobby decided to sell his IROC, Tony's name instinctively arose. Zucci cut an "as is" deal for his future financial burden and Tony blinked. The chance to drive an IROC around the Boulevard at such a young age was simply unheard of. The deal would allow Zucci to knock off some alimony as well. Tony Baloney was making a name for himself in leaps and bounds. "I just wanna ride," Tony would put in his yearbook shortly thereafter, "and Ozzy fuckin' rules! Love you Ma."

•

The *IROC-Z* purrs southward, its sexy curvature slicing through an inland headwind. The night is starry and keg-colored grey. Traffic is moderate and tedious: Route 128 has only two lanes for half the distance to Boston. Still, by quarter to ten, Tony Baloney's passing the Liberty Tree Mall at exit 24, just a few miles before the road opens into four corridors. A valley of automobiles collects like silt about the concrete landscape. The parking lots of Liberty Tree Mall and Peabody Shopping Center swell towards rusted guardrails. Here the girl pool is fertile for flirting. However, malls are for children marching with embarrassment ten steps in front of mommy and daddy, hoping not to be seen. Clubs are where the big kids play.

The crew pauses behind the sloping, spotless windshield as Boston's skyline comes into focus. The Hub's incredibly diversified population is bursting at the seams. The Cuzzins sense the hum of humanity. Crystals traipse through their bloodstreams. This is the Promiseland.

•

Tony Baloney refuses to answer the ringing cellphone in his glove compartment. He often leaves messages for Lorenzo Pimento to give anyone inquiring his whereabouts. But this Fiesta Eve, one can assume, a phone call from Gloucester would be pointless and distracting. Besides, the bass on the stereo system could drown out low-flying aircraft. That's another peculiarity of cruising Cuzzins: treble low, bass high.

Thousands of windowlights from skyscrapers and street corners checker the horizon like hovering fireflies. Traffic congests. Tony's crew stops in front of a club. Let the carnage begin.

•

The first crucial step towards a love connection is zeroing a target and making successful eye contact. Cuzzes must be careful not to look like loners pathetically pressing their noses against the glass of an ammo shop. Remember: A preoccupation with nothing is a Cuz's most prominent characteristic. It requires supreme confidence, (though it's hard looking cool when a bouncer twice your size is holding your limp wrist and stamping your hand in the cold rain.) That's why the bar is where the real game begins.

Once inside, a ground zero must be established near the beer. Bars are like altars: There is great reverence for all things behind them, and a dignified presence from standing before them. With dozens of guys looking for prizes, it takes a lot of fight from a cohesive team to gain a bar seat. Obtaining a barstool is like pissing on a pine tree. A territory is established.

Whether seated or standing, once drinks are ordered the navigation process begins. There are three hotspots Cuzzins automatically pivot to for scoping: the exit, the dance floor, and the ladies room. At one particular locality in Boston, a staple of the Cuzzins' Keepah menu, the heart of the club is a large square bar, with the dance floor, bathrooms and only exit at the far end of the building. Without thinking, Cuzzins furiously look to see if this is a place to invest cherished time. The dance floor needs to be hopping, the alcohol should pour like rain, as should the lines through the door and towards the restrooms.

Contacts can be made without speaking. If music is too loud or crowds too boisterous, a Cuz must rely on instincts and animal magnetism, something he'll gladly do. One may become separated from others: Cuzzins are prepared to fend for themselves. "I'd ratha be out on my own," says Frankie Vermann. "I don't wanna hafta rely on my crew to get me Keepahs. Besides, why would I wanna compete with my boys when I'm out lookin' for a piece of action? Know what I'm sayin'?" But Tony, Meatballeyes, Johnny, Vito and Rigga know how each other operates. Everyone is allowed space. Since clubs are dark and exploding with strobe lights, contacts can also be made hastily. The typical scene inside a Beantown nightclub is very dark, very loud, very sweaty, very drunk. You may see the outline of a breast here, some lipgloss there, but by closing time, when the lights come on, sloppy guesswork may land you one hell of a beating from the crew on the ride home.

If one of the boys is out on his own, he is in charge of keeping himself wasted. But in most cases that does not happen until the crew shares a couple rounds. A round of poorly mixed drinks in Boston could cost forty bucks. Cuzzins don't want to waste cold hard cash on vodka tonics when there's a BU undergrad with a history of passing out just waiting for someone to buy her a fifth banana daiquiri. Some guys will wait for everyone else to buy a round before splitting from the group. But that sort of stuff will inevitably come back to haunt them. A solid but fruitless night in the capital may run each Cuz a couple hundred bucks—not counting after-hours charades. In fact, the biggest squabbles amongst crewmen are not over who owes who a beer, it's what are they going to do when back in the car.

The Boston bar and club scene winds down near mid-morning, so if expectations are not immediately met, it's off to another section of the city. There's a method to successful cruising, a measured process. Crews make several stops any given night. (An especially fidgety captain, Tony undoubtedly flushed his Cuzzes through several establishments.) With imaginary research we've learned Tony's luckless crew left their first stop almost immediately.

Wounded, they saunter back to the car, assume the same seating arrangement, grab zazeets or a slice of pizza, and eat outside, all the while looking for dings and scratches. Tony checks the wax coating, notes the gas tank. He listens for messages on his phone. His cellphone is the hottest model on the market, so a quick call to Gloucester about what may be brewing can be done with little worry of interference. No matter the time of night, there's always a Cuz at the Boulevard.

By midnight, crowds from Fenway and the Theater District are partying in full force. It is truly summer. Tony's Camaro is full of drunken Cuzzins with volcanic hormones. If the ratio of males to females becomes shockingly dim, anything with two teats and a bucket will qualify. The stereo plays a little softer, the cooler's a little emptier. A delicate trickle of coeds spritzing Landsdowne Street offers promise of what lies behind the Green Monster. That familiar dance club throb thumps from inside the concrete, and an ocean-blue *IROC-Z* sneaks ever so slightly towards a place to park.

•

Young people brainlessly form lines under awnings and atop asphalt streets. From the sky, Boston must look like an ant farm. In this student-infested area, surrounding establishments provide overanxious singles a sliver of hope.

The Cuzzins plod out the *IROC-Z* and into formation again, with heavier heads and lighter wallets. It's warm and sticky, any vests or jackets the men might have been wearing are now in the car. Game faces are activated, and the guys aren't even out of the parking lot. At this time of night, around such traffic, a return to Gloucester for last call is out of the question.

From where they've parked it is possible to see a panoramic view of bars, pool halls, dance clubs and breweries. The Cuzzins can comb either side of any street and reel themselves in the direction they came now or after Boston shuts down. Johnny takes off to secure a place in line, ready to schmooze.

Chasing Schoolies in the Landsdowne Street area behind Fenway Park is easier than finding Keepahs in the uppity pockets of the city. Some dance clubs offer "18 and Over" nights. This presents a bevy of opportunities for experienced Cuzzins to impress the impressionable. The "18-Plus" crowd brings its particular sort of danger though: They have little money and are less apt to leave familiar areas next to college housing. To make matters worse, the young ladies may be experimenting with foreign substances or are away from high school boyfriends for the first time. If a Cuz were to hook-up, he'd have to do so with unwanted responsibilities.

Regardless, someone could find himself between uninhibited college sophomores, and even the most cynical Cuz would be willing to listen to an hour and a half of Tori Amos to get laid. Plus, perks everywhere. A Schoolie could have several roommates or a free-parking pass: Things a guy needs. Keeps the crew happy too.

•

A Schoolie tangled in a Cuz's web of seduction emits several telltale symptoms. After absorbing one devastating pick-up line after the other, her eyes suddenly become glassy. This is when the rest of the available crew comes in, a circle of sharks, surrounding the object of affection. Overwhelmed, she smiles idiotically, head nodding like a bobbing-doll. *Wanna 'notha drink? I think ya' legs ah pretty. Wanna 'notha drink? Yuh eyes is like springtime. Wanna 'notha drink? Come inside my cah. Wanna 'notha drink? I'll let ya touch my body.* Pow! She's entranced.

On a great night, perhaps the Schoolie's friends enter the circle to find what all the fuss is about. There *are* instances when Schoolies come to their senses. The sting of defeat affects the crew only momentarily. They quickly regroup, and twirl like a twister 'cross the dance floor. But the circle is rarely broken. The washboard stomachs, those neon-white teeth, that throat-restricting aftershave, the thick ropes of gold chains—she's caught.

The occasional female *with* a conscience may bolt for a bathroom or run to her straight-laced boyfriend before the circle closes. It's then a Cuz's position gets defensive. "We drive too fuggin' fah from Glosta," says Lorenzo Pimento's longtime coolerman. "If I'm out in a cah for two owiz, I sure as hell ain't goin' home with just my right fu'in hand."

Quality Cuzzins keep track of hotspots. They're the ones who tell you where the keg's going. They know if Jenna Jameson's stripping in Rhode Island. They change flat tires and radiator coolant. They make the phone calls. They drink Old Milwaukee *two cans* at a time.

The best crews can each net a girl on a good trip. The most successful venture anyone on the Boulevard can remember is nine girls for four guys. (That's without paying for it.) That was at a cheerleading competition the autumn after the Factory football team reached the state Super Bowl for the first time. Even the placekicker got laid. That's why guys play football, and that's why they end up at the Boulevard in IROCs when the season's done.

For every sweet harvest though, there are numberless dry evenings. Most trips do end in frustration. Premium Keepahs cover the North Shore, from Gloucester to Boston and all points in between. But you have to find your booty before pale ale-drinking businessmen dangle platinum credit cards before the eyes of hypnotized admirers. Even the best captains miscalculate where the action is.

In all fairness, there are periods where times are tough, such as during final exams or three-day blizzards. A crew's mettle is tested when the ladies aren't around, and desperation does noxious things to the minds of men. No one knows why, but when Cuzzins go weeks between hook-ups, they turn practically rabid. Millions of unreleased sperm swim frenetically through the loins, unleashing a powerful energy surge. It's hara-kiri, the depths a love-starved Cuz will sink to. In such inconsolable times, garages are cleaned and cleared for weight benches, goatees grown and maintained, sports trivia flies at local bars, adult video rentals skyrocket, and old girlfriends are hounded and harassed. In prolonged spells, grown men have been known to compete with neighborhood dogs for the chance to dry-hump street signs and fire hydrants.

•

Through the first few hours off the island, the Cuzzins snarl and prowl and snarl some more. In chillier climes, the boys might resort to J. Crew sweater vests or leather jackets. But the clubs are steamy, and inadvertent flexing is running rampant. Strobes and lasers reflect well off sweat. Tested veterans use this to their advantage, and Tony's crew probably does too, but not before another quick timeout for more zazeets.

To Cuzzins, Boston is an exotic and erotic wonderland. Its character is very different from the homeyness of Gloucester and other North Shore communities. Each city along 128 does have peculiarities, but generally its features are interchangeable. Not Boston. That's a world away. Your awareness is heightened when you leave the suburbs for the city. You're no longer cutting through familiar cemeteries and backyards on the way home from bars. You're praying you have enough loose change and conversational Haitian for the midnight cab rides. No Cuz could ever slip in his own vomit in front of Old Timer's and think he's behind the Prudential Center. Gloucester has an West End. Boston has a fucking Chinatown.

Tony's leading the boys around the corner of Landsdowne to the nearest sausage vendor. Down the street by Boston Billiards, he sees Frankie Vermann in his grey Cadillac *Seville 1* having a smoke. Tony and Frankie used to play baseball together, and each idiot actually kept track of how many RBI's he had. They communicate like primates with a series of well-versed hand signals and crotch grabs. Every now and then they bump into each other when cruising, but never talk much. Dueling Cuzzins don't socialize with each other. They waste time in front of the Greasy Pole and chickenfight each other all day long, but once removed from the Boulevard, their only motive is to talk to the fairer sex. Both men have been known to entirely ignore one another in a bar.

A few minutes later, Vermann and his crew offer a couple Schoolies a ride. As they drive by Tony and the boys, Vermann promises to call and make plans to booze for Fiesta. The *Seville 1* spits through the maze of avenues and trolley tracks to find a highway. There is little night left. The air is filled with sweet scents of peppers and onions. Frankie Vermann is heading into Glosta for last call at the Rhumb Line. It's been one long year since last Fiesta.

If walking into Old Timers or House of Mitch is like walking into seventh grade study hall, the Rhumb Line is like being trapped in the girls' bathroom at Rockport High School. It's a tiny joint with live music and a horseshoe-shaped bar. Kids from money suburbs with no stomach for downtown Glosta love the Rhumb Line. They can jack-off to Grateful Dead cover bands, fascinate over drinking dingleberry-flavored pale ales, and braid each other's pubic hair. Patrons are advised to bring an extra lung for breathing.

•

Vermann's Cadillac *Seville 1* holds an awful lot of cargo, be it Cuzzins or Keepahs. But he's very impatient, and like a lot of Gloucesterites, gets anxious when away from the womb for an extended period of time. Older and wiser than the others, Frankie certainly knows 128, but his head is on the island. "Some guys fu'in think they can walk in any place and grab anyone they want," says Vermann. "But ya neva know who's gotcha back outta town. There's a lotta fuggin' wackos out there. Fuck that. Even if you do bring a girl home, you gotta drive her back the next day. Fuck that. I know a kid that got slapped because he dropped some girl off at the train station instead of drivin' her to Boston. If that happened to me I'd be like, `You can go fug a fuggin'.'"

Sure enough, exactly as Vermann leaves, a street fight between competing crews spills into the parking lot. Someone may have mimicked an opposing crewman's trademark strut: Unacceptable! In mere seconds knuckleheads gather and multiply. Like spinning coins the men rattle about, spewing obscenities and grappling collars. The Cuzzins investigate. They're given hard looks and unspoken challenges. Soon enough, they're locking forearms and struggling for position. They weren't looking for a fight, but the undulating mass is consuming. One minute they're wiping mustard off their chins, the next they're panicked over the safety of the Camaro. Some zippers and class rings get dangerously close to the bodypaint, and the car sways helplessly, but the Cuzzins fend them off. Girlfriends scream and plead for a truce. The fight downgrades into a staring contest.

When the rough stuff subsides, Tony checks for damages. His cellphone dropped from the glove compartment, but containers of hair gel didn't budge. Tony calls Frankie Vermann to make sure his phone still works. He explains what happened, yelling within earshot of the combatants. "Fuggin' idiots!" Tony shouts. "I should bust some fuggin' heads!"

In a confusing whirlwind, the Cuzzins reboard the *IROC-Z*. They babble and curse to Vermann's *Seville 1* about how the fight may have started. Frankie doesn't like what he hears. The *IROC-Z* is a delicate machine and Tony's a bit of a hothead. The moral code of every crew: *Anything goes but—YOU DO NOT SCRATCH THE FUCKING HOT ROD!* "I couldn't tell those guys to calm down," says Vermann. "No one had a girl yet. For five Cuzzes that's a lot of frustration. It's what we call a CTS, a Critical Testicular Situation."

The *IROC-Z* cruises along the side streets of the North End, searching for pubs ignoring curfew. As far as Frankie Vermann can tell, the Camaro's voyage thus far has been less than fruitful. Cuzzins can't stay away from the island too long. Attitudes get cold, beer gets warm. Somebody has to get a girl—fast. Sexual anxiety has almost reached a Code Red status. The widely praised scouting report on Keepahs, Schoolies, Medheads and the like (memorized like Scripture by each and every Cuz), can be crunched into a ball and tossed out the window. After one o'clock, they scourge the holes-in-the-walls for green-haired music students, varsity softball teams playing foosball, anything. All other crews are in Gloucester at bars or beaches. Lorenzo Pimento is loitering in front of McT's Tavern. Frankie Vermann is outside the Rhumb Line. A group of friends including Yo-Yo OneNut and Joe Tomatoes stand in a circle at Old Timer's, nursing their last drinks before being ushered outdoors.

    Tony's IROC is driving god-only-knows-where. His cellphone is out of range now. The Cuzzins are drunk and aggravated. All they wanted were a couple good Boston stories for Fiesta. This has devolved into a salvaging mission.

6

The Riggiz of the Road

Frankie Vermann's Cadillac *Seville 1* leaves the Rhumb Line just after one o'clock Fiesta Thursday morning for a kegger at the private side of Wingaersheek Beach. He's chasing Schoolies and high school seniors and having a slammer trip. He's even lost and forgot about a phone number some little Medhead handed him in Boston. His car is parked with other familiar vehicles of the Boulevard fleet. The partygoers revel around a small fire in the middle of a white dune.

At the beach the topic of conversation naturally shifts to horrible sexcapades remembered. A popular story the boys pass around is the sad tale of Chinstrap Calzone. Calzone was an exceptional football player for Gloucester High back in the day. So good, in fact, he was courted and subsequently offered scholarships from such athletic juggernauts as Michigan and Purdue. He was the talk of the town, even grand-marshaled the Horribles Parade his senior year.

Legend tells us Calzone skipped off the island alone one evening and, perhaps in the same fashion that got the crew of the *IROC-Z*, met a rather large woman and bedded her. To make a long story longer, she retained his seed, a Cuz's worst nightmare. On top of that, the girl must have been on top of Chinstrap. He threw out his back. End of football career. End of scholarship. End of Calzone.

Picture the damage being done this Fiesta Eve.

The Cuzzins could be experiencing exactly what Calzone suffered. It's a heartbreaking and dangerous scene to imagine: knee-deep in stretched skin, paralyzed by fright. Think: If a thousand-pound sports car couldn't handle such stress, what could a skinny Guinea do? "IROCs have solid shocks and suspension," notes Bobby Zucci. "Cuzzins have gold chains and four pounds of back hair."

•

Like most Boulevard creatures, Vermann started cruising before he earned a learner's permit. He was driving an IROC before age 20 and got the Caddy when his landscaping job took off. He's got a sometime-girlfriend from Rockport and does oil changes and tune-ups for beer. Buying a Cadillac at his advanced age was a logical progression. That's why he's outside Gloucester more than most captains. Terrorizing town in sports cars is a young man's game. Vermann doesn't need the headache of worrying about gas money or delegating coolermen or shotgunner anymore. He's had an impressive career. He hasn't waited in line for a keg cup in years. Hosts hand him beers. Nowadays, Vermann only shows his face every now and then, at a class reunion perhaps, just to let other Cuzzins know who really is the *Caddy Daddy*.

Of course, as time passes, the more one cruises the more likely one is to get hitched. Those kinds of hopeless opportunities to knock Cuzzes out of the dating game are everlasting: high school sweethearts, college girlfriends, bitter divorcees—the kind of women that sap the strength from Cuzzes by sucking them into commitment. The gene pool takes a beating here. More Glosta folk are distantly related to each other per capita, than in any of America's other "first seaports." A player in his twilight like Vermann may have better luck maintaining his Scrotum Pole status by eventually settling down with someone from outside Route 128.

Vermann knows a lot of guys who never thought they'd crawl home after spending time away. Guys who enjoyed college campus life, maybe got good work, maybe saw an Asian for the first time. Then—bang! As soon as they get comfortable in a new setting—the magnet under the Bridge draws them up 128 again.

You can't take the Cuzzins out of Gloucester, or the Gloucester out of Cuzzins.

•

From information gathered, Tony Baloney's having a bad trip. A place to party isn't all Tony has on his mind at this point. The ice in the cooler has melted, and most liquor stores are closed. Normally, a cooler of beer is enough for an overnight excursion. But it seems as though the *IROC-Z* has been riding in circles. As each hour passes, so do the quality Keepahs. The best way to compensate is to find the largest crowd within reach. Push in or pull out? It's a dilemma that's plagued homesick Cuzzins for years.

And what about the crew? They're boozed and belligerent. Moreover, hours of drinking, sweating and perfuming have a malodorous effect on the car's interior. By the time the cranky Cuzzins come back to Gloucester, nobody will want to see each other until Sunday. Of course, no one wants to agitate the captain and Tony's got a reputation for being a bit of a loose cannon. But when situations are *so* bleak, someone, *anyone* needs to deliver a viable suggestion. If they're gonna spend Fiesta two tablespoons lighter, they better start cracking.

After five hours on the road, the crew has only a couple phone numbers amongst them. When Lorenzo Pimento's cellphone is finally in range, he calls the *IROC-Z*. In a ramble, Tony mentions how defeated the boys feel and devises a list of last-ditch efforts he's thinking of trying since he's already miles from Gloucester.

Boulevard buddies help each other out from time to time, and Pimento thinks the party at Wingaersheek could last until dawn. But from the seashell echo surrounding Tony's voice, Lorenzo figures the captain is cupping the receiver, perhaps shouldering a wall before his crew.

Pimento: Hey Tone, it's just me and you now, Cuz. Where you thinkin' of goin'?
Baloney: Some Schoolie gave me this address—
Pimento: Oh Jesus! Not a Schoolie!
Baloney: Listen Cuz! There's a huge rave in Poppycock Cove—
Pimento: Poppycock Cove?! Don't you know what's in Poppycock Cove?
Baloney: Course I know Cuz. I figya the soona we get there the betta.
Pimento: It's Fiesta, Tone! Why don't ya just call it a trip and head in, Cuz?
Baloney: Call it a trip? Fug that! We got nothin' Larry! Nothin'! I'm gonna finish my booze and hand out the squids.
Pimento: Tony! You're goin' right into the eye of the monstah!!!

What Pimento means is that the Cuzzes are headed into a heap of trouble; that their mental compasses are spinning out of control. Their chauvinism and machismo has been stripped raw. Their aesthetic preferences, which takes years of obtuse thinking to manifest, have been tossed by the wayside. There will be no swimsuit models, bellydancers or gold-medal gymnasts to kiss on this night. Pimento pictures Tony Baloney mentally burning a stack of *Penthouse* magazines, and frantically rummaging through page after page of *Sweeter Cakes and Cookies*, and *Today's Milkshake*. What's even more frightening is that once Tony finds an orca in a halter-top, the crew will have no choice but to follow suit.

Once they hang up, Tony and Lorenzo may not speak again until Sunday's seine boat races off Pavilion Beach.

Tony peers at the back of his Marlboros for jotted directions to the rave. Though this crew hasn't been there before, Poppycock Cove is nearby and residence to many coeds. It may be out of the way, but it's a chance the Cuzzins are going to have to take.

•

Like all sporty cars, the fragile condition of an IROC supplements its allure. Bobby Zucci bought one directly off the blessed assembly line and souped that baby to levels never dreamed attainable, from the stereo system to the breakaway shag rug. At the hint of a stiff steering column or squeaky brakeline, Zucci would repair the car himself or have it sent to a much-respected mechanic. The cost of constant upkeep was never an issue. Tony bought the car from Zucci and kept it in excellent condition. He even stuck a parade ribbon with St. Peter's likeness to the dashboard for sacred decoration. From the beating it takes and the mileage tacked on, this particular IROC model held up awfully well. It would take a helluva hammering to put her on the shelf.

If there is one gripe however, one that may be on Tony's mind this night so far from home, it concerns the transmission fluid. For some reason Zucci, Tony or their respective mechanics fail to put their fingers on, the car goes through an extraordinary amount of transmission fluid. Once, fluid began to drip under the car's belly, leaving in its wake a trail of smoke so thick Tony couldn't see his adorable reflection in the backshield. This is very dangerous. Transmission fluid is the most flammable fluid in an automobile—worse than gasoline. But a couple weeks in the shop (and a thousand bucks) convinced Tony the problem had been solved. The question of fragility hadn't emerged since.

"If the transmission's leakin' you're in real trouble," says Zucci. "The cah stahts to grind like a salami. You can always tell. Then you have to pull right ova and get the hell out. If you push it too long you might shoot it to hell and blow the whole damn thing. You shouldn't have to keep an extra quart in the cah at all times.

But that's the riggiz of the road. Ah cahs spend their whole lives on the road. It's kinda honorable to have 'em die there."

•

Bobby Zucci's not the most popular guy in Gloucester. He has the distinction for pawning his lemons to first-time buyers. But the man knows cars. And he knows how to get them. As a boy, Zucci would attach lawnmower engines to scooters and go-carts. At the Factory, he'd skip Trig or History to sneak into the Vocational Department garage. What put him on the map though, was one of the most storied and appreciated pranks in Gloucester High School history. During the night of the Senior Class Scavenger Hunt, Zucci led a handful of friends in disassembling the principal's Toyota, bit by bit. The principal was off campus, tagging along with police in hopes of cutting down on the evening's criminal mischief. Zucci's clan spent the rest of the night frantically reassembling the car until it was back in working condition by the time the principal arrived at daybreak, *inside the high school lobby!* That made a big splash.

Years later, another Factory incident would muddy the Rat Rocket's repute. One of the first IROCs he sold was to a student preparing to lead the senior class parade of cars to a ball field called the Oval for a champagne breakfast (that's a keg party *before* the schoolday begins). It's a tradition of seniors on the last day of classes. What made that year's breakfast so tantalizing was that most of the cops were too busy having coffee with construction crews replacing water pipes at the Back Shore. Anyway, as the parade careened through the Boulevard, horns honking, streamers waving, kids hanging out the windows, the lead car, the Camaro, inexplicably broke down. Something about an alternator. The confusion and commotion attracted the police, and the parade and party were canceled. The kids with the keg ended up sweeping trash at the fire station for a month as part of a community service payback plan. That kind of thing sticks in your craw.

Now, the IROC Zucci sold Tony was Zucci's in the first place. No one, not even Tony, doubted the durability of that particular Camaro. It was a horse. But every now and then, the horse would cramp.

•

Despite the rough start, the guys in Tony's car remain upbeat. They may be lost and low on booze, but the rave sounds like a great idea. If that failed, there was always Wingaersheek.

However, raves are wildly unpredictable. Everyone's on a ton of Xtasy, it's pitch black, and as Pimento warns, "hotter than two mice humpin' in a wool sock." Most importantly, it's all-inclusive. *Everyone* gets in. This time of year, late in June and close to July 4th weekend, college kids are home, high schoolers through with finals, and power-drinkers are priming for another holiday. A late night rave is an open invitation for the uninhibited to make hay. The Cuzzins know full well once the door closes behind them they are at the mercy of the crowd.

The trek to Poppycock will momentarily have the crew heading towards Gloucester. But they will quickly leave I-95 north and venture onto some never before seen byways. A missed exit or street sign could spell doom.

As the *IROC-Z* veers through Greater Boston's sidestreets, Tony harks back to his conversation with Lorenzo Pimento. Lorenzo asked if Tony was sure about going to the rave. If not, the Bigfoot *America* crew would wait for the guys at Wingaersheek. Tony handed the phone to Meatballeyes, who quickly waved Lorenzo off. Then he locked the phone in the glove compartment. It will be the last contact anyone from the island has with the *IROC-Z*. Somewhere out there, a deejay is spinning, an audience is rocking, and five lonely girls have Cuzzins in their sights.

7

The Fuller Squish

The human body is nearly 80% water. The human Cuz is nearly 80% emotionally retarded ego. So there's a certain denial in hooking-up with the unexpected, especially when the unexpected is nowhere to be found on any scouting report. But if you're on the schnide, you gotta do what you gotta do. It's like being drafted for war. Take one last drag, lock, load, and march. Sure, you won't be able to look your buddies in the eyes, and you'll get a lifetime of shit for your troubles, but you've knocked one out, and now the healing can begin.

Once you've slept with your first obscenely overweight partner, it becomes much easier to slump into a second. If you stare at a Cuz depraved of nookie long enough, you can virtually see his standards drop. Some Cuzzins are awfully smug about never having to stoop. They make a point of saying how they could *never* do such a thing. Then you don't see or hear from them for three weeks . . .

The further from Gloucester you are, the easier it is to amplify courage and push thoughts of jeering Cuzzins to the vast recesses of your mind. What are the chances of someone from town finding out? If your closest friends are semi-reliable, you just might get away with it. Tony doesn't worry about who may or may not be at the rave. He's been through a million scenarios on a thousand different occasions. Same shit, different day.

There are certain things an accomplished Cuz does to avoid the unavoidable. Whether the guys in Tony's car, especially the youngsters in back, know what to do remains to be seen. Tony's picked up vapid-but-happening chicks his whole life. But some Cuzzins think their shit smells like Christmas pie; that their presence alone drives undesirable women away, leaving sex-crazed Keepahs to fend for themselves. It's a perilously false sense of security. Fat-bottomed girls are everywhere, people. And they need lovin' too.

Good friends do everything in their power to save a fat-trapped crewman. They offer air bags and safety flares from the other side of the bar, summon ex-girlfriends to bail him out, or smack his nose with a newspaper, grab him by the ear, and drag him outside. (If the Cuz actually seems *interested*, he is put through a battery of tests such as eye exams, word association, and reflex checks to assure the others he is in control of his faculties.)

There's always a lookout designated to "check the scene" before crews commit to any bar or party. Only Tony and Meatballeyes have substantial off-the-island experience, so they are the ones ultimately accountable for what they get into.

•

Meatballeyes reappears from the front of an abandoned warehouse where the rave is rollicking. All he's got is stuff the four guys in the IROC don't want to hear: The booze is almost gone, the deejay stopped playing, and Medheads are looking for quick fixes. A door waving to and fro reveals a glimpse every second or so of the partygoers inside. They ain't exactly pretty. Ain't exactly small. Meatballeyes doesn't want to tell the crew what they already fear: This is a Feta Alpha Tau party.

Feta Alpha Tau is a popular New England sorority. Sisters don't join this sorority for academic or athletic reasons. They are there to congregate and vegetate. Notorious party-crashers, Taus are neither shy nor quiet, always traveling in thundering herds. But something else needs to be said to further explain these illustrious sorority sisters. They are not your average bear. There is pleasantly plump, charmingly chunky, and adorably unctuous. Then there's whatever the hell the Taus are.

Humans possessing such amazing, gravity-defying girth that villagers in remote Chinese provinces are said to feel tremors during Tau dance marathons. NASA currently has unmanned spacecraft probing and circulating a Tau in Dos Ricardos, Texas. When working with Taus, orthodontists, barbers, and eyeglass salesmen must rent Sherpa guides to reach their destinations.

And still, the most fascinating aspect of Tau lifestyle is their unabashed pride in their appearance. Let there be no pity party for these gals. They'd no sooner rip your head off (and nibble on the sweet parts) than absorb a sorrowful gaze. If some poor soul were to speak comforting words lamenting a Tau's condition, he would not receive a sweet smile of gratitude, but more likely a bloated hoagie across his neck.

It's a dog eat dog world. And if you're overcome by a giant shadow someday and can feel garlic powder and basil being sprinkled on your body, I'd run.

Now regrettably, Meatballeyes's timid entrance did not go unnoticed. With each flap of the door, the Cuzzins see the Taus and the Taus see the IROC. Tony may call the entire trip a wash and bolt for the highway, or take his chances with what's behind Door #1. The fact that he is glutted with testosterone and low on beer must weigh in his decision.

Tony: Alright. Let's do it.
Rigga: Um, wait a minute Tone . . . Things don't look so good in there.
Tony: Don't look good, Rigga? You wanna go home to suntin' betta? Go ahead.
Rigga: It's not that Tone. I heard about girls like them.
Tony: Oh you did, did you?

Rigga: I seen them downtown before—they did in my uncle. He called one of 'em Haystacks . . .
Johnny: Yeah Tone, whaddaya say we head back for Fiesta?
Tony: Head back? We're *Glostamen*, aren't we?
Johnny: Yeah we're Glostamen—
Tony: And Glostamen don't turn back. Do we?
Meatballeyes: Vito's uncle sure didn't.
Tony: You're fuggin' right he didn't.
Rigga: Yeah Tone, but now look at him. He talks to parkin' meters. The state makes him wear a bib.
Tony: Y'know, I'm lookin' around here and all I see is a bunch of loozahs! I didn't come all the way down here in my Baby Blue to waste fuggin' gas money. Did you?
Rigga: No . . .
Tony: Now I *know* my man Meatballeyes is in.
Meatballeyes: Damn straight Cuz—
Tony: And I ain't goin' home til I get me some—like a *real* Cuz.
Johnny: Tony . . . they're *huge*.
Tony: *Tony is no longer listening. Tony is now fishing. Tony wants satisfaction. We're Glostamen, right? Right?* Ask Vito. He's kept his mouth shut.

•

Many a Cuz has settled for a big girl before, but Vito Ditalini's escapades have called extra attention to his initials. He's a big guy, always has been, but years before finding free-weights he was rather portly. He's no Kory Curcuru now, but at least he can run to first base without making a beeline to the oxygen tent. His big frame naturally introduced him to big girls, and as time passed, Vito got used to the extra cushion. Once, he and a couple friends were partying with three Glochicks in his parent's basement. Two of the girls were thin, the other full of donuts. It's no doubt his two buds were scared shitless over who they would end up with. Get this: Vito took the donut dream! Didn't faze him a bit. Taking one for the team like that may merit chants of, "V.D.!" now and then, but Vito rarely gets any *real* grief.

•

"We've all done it before," says Frankie Vermann. "You suck in ya chest, take one huge gulp and go for it. Fuck. It fuggin' sucks, Cuz."

•

The boys are walking straight into Satan's wheelhouse. For the next half-hour the rave is eerily quiet. The only sign of recognition they receive is from a group of wallflowers, more wall than flowers, loafing in a corner. As the minutes pass, the Taus drinks get smaller, and space between the Cuzzins begins to shrink. They eye over the guys with cautious sensuality, like raccoons creeping in a trash bin. One girl lifts her skirt up a touch, revealing a thigh so white, massive and veiny, it looks like a Montana roadmap. Another gradually slides her tongue across her braces, plucking out party mix kernel by kernel. Yet another playfully elevates and rests her pump on a stool. The top of her foot is so meaty, it looks as though her ankles are roasting Jiffy Pop. When one girl returns to her sisters to refresh margaritas, they strike. The Cuzzes huddle and hold onto each other, as a deep, dark shadow slowly rises from the tips of their toes, above their Meester Joes, beyond their chains of gold, until all surrounding light and sound is quashed. It's a molar eclipse.

It's a strange predicament. The Cuzzins stutter through introductions the way peglegs stamp out brushfire. Crews gauge the danger of such encounters by the sound of giddy girls laughing together. A nervous chuckle means no matter what Cuzzins say, Taus will act impressed. An ordinary laugh means Taus feel invited to get closer. A booming, thigh-slapping frenzy means Taus know they're in, and any resistance by Cuzzins would be futile. Lorenzo

Pimento once had an eighth-grader in his Bigfoot crowing so idiotically, he swore off lurking around American Legion-sponsored youth dances for months.

    Soon enough there is a lull in the conversation. But Taus can fill lulls like apples in a pig snout. They don't have the luxury shark-eyed Keepahs have: posing like potted plants, enduring one moronic pick-up line after the other. Taus search and destroy. And tonight they have a direct mission. These Taus are *so* glad Cuzzins arrived, by the time another pitcher of margaritas is ordered, the guys are secretly rubbing rosary beads.

    Tony's got a wild look in his eye. When bouncers start sweeping the floor, he leads his men outdoors. He may try to find 128 and track down Pimento or Vermann. For whatever reason though, Tony's mind is settled. Perhaps he's content with surprising the guys. The crew believes they're going to Wingaersheek or the Boulevard. Lorenzo Pimento in his Bigfoot *America*, Frankie Vermann in his Cadillac *Seville 1*, and Yo-Yo OneNut, some way or another, will find their way to the Man-at-the-Wheel by sunrise. Only Lorenzo knows where the ocean-blue *IROC-Z* might be. "When I heard it was the Taus I got a wickit sceary feelin'," admits Pimento.

    Frankie Vermann is less sympathetic. "They knew what they wuz goin' afta," he says. "Doin' a big one's like goin' to work. Monday mornin' rolls around, you just do it. Punch in. Punch the fug out. Fuggit."

•

    The shuffle out the warehouse and down the driveway is agonizingly slow. Each Tau has paired herself with a Cuz. Not much is said as the *IROC-Z* comes into view. This signifies one thing only: something unspeakable is about to happen.

    Everyone is piling into the Camaro now, six in back, four in front. The extra weight is burdensome, unexpected, and unwelcome. The cooler is emptied and discarded. The *IROC-Z* is a balloon about to burst. In order to fit, each Cuz must have a

Tau on his lap, even the driver. Tony labors to find his way off the property. The Cuzzins take turns joking around, trying anything to hide their terror. It takes a good sense of humor to get through something like this, though laughter seems inappropriate. To a man, these are the most intimidating, unnerving girls they've ever been around. For the first time in their lives, the Cuzzins consider the negatives of promiscuity.

Meanwhile at Wingaersheek Beach, Lorenzo Pimento and his crew are so disturbed over what the *IROC-Z* has gotten into, they chuckle and cringe at the same time. Pimento emptily clenches his keg cup. Like most Boulevard skippers, he doesn't eliminate the possibility that someone besides Tony may have hooked-up, and the captain is simply waiting on a friend. If that's the case, Tony's probably sitting at the wheel drunk or stoned or sleeping. Other Cuzzins might be in back, wondering aloud Vito's odds for Friday's Greasy Pole.

"I figya," says Bobby Zucci, wincing as he imagines what might have happened with ten people in a Camaro, "the Taus have the stereo on real loud, singin' along with the music. They're probably so big the guys can't see each utha. One of ums yappin' ordiz at Tony, tellin' him where to drive. Every now and then Meatballeyes might ask if the girls have somethin' important to do the next mornin'. Olda Cuzzins know how to get out of shit like that. The kids in back are probably quivarin' like the cah . . . all that weight."

Whether the *IROC-Z* holds all ten or not, it takes a bad beating. Bobby Zucci, thumbing a tear from his cheek, gravely motions the Sign of the Cross.

•

The *IROC-Z* is built to feel every inch of asphalt, meaning it rides low to the ground. It's supposed to lift a bit in headwinds and hydroplane over puddles. But hauling 1200 pounds of Fritos and cake mix is for flatbeds and forklifts. Whenever large amounts of weight shift, the car sags and sways, and Tony must power-steer significantly to avoid guardrails and newspaper stands. An IROC riding with so much weight simply aches with pain.

If Tony's gonna drive awhile he'll risk popping a rim or scraping the fender. To make matters worse, the Taus are punchdrunk, giddy, and flopping like mackerel. At some point while toiling through the back roads of Greater Boston, Tony Baloney must have decided his *IROC-Z* had had enough.

If there's anything that keeps a Cuz from bringing a trophy chick all the way home, it's having driving instructions shouted in his face. If one of the Taus were to suggest a sharp swerve into an all-night diner or motel, Tony would have to fight his way through the lard to keep on course. With all mirrors blocked, only median strips and breakdown lanes could guide him.

But Tony's run though this drill many times, and harking back to the advice of yesteryear's captains, a dumpy motel is the safest place to hide from the public. Either way, this radical change in direction is the moment of truth. The window of opportunity to escape has narrowed immensely. Submitting to Taus proves the crew is willing. As soon as they pull over, there's no time to check for damage, just straight to the sheets.

That afternoon, they could have decided to stay and watch wet T-shirts and air guitarists. A few hours ago, they could have followed Frankie Vermann up 128. A few minutes ago, they could have boogied out the warehouse and scrambled to the getaway car. Now, hundreds of pounds of tipsy sorority girls have their arms around them—and they ain't letting go. No one, not Tony Baloney, not Johnny Ziti, knows what will happen next.

•

It's been more than twenty minutes since Lorenzo Pimento raised Tony's phone. Maybe they're closing a strip joint, or smoking a joint and splitting a bucket of chicken fingers, Lorenzo thinks. Maybe the guys are in Gloucester, or maybe Tony's phone is sapped. Car trouble seems too terrible a thought to think. Pimento won't allow himself to do so.

When the remaining Cuzzins convene at the Boulevard for a nightcap, Pimento tries calling again. The phone rings, which means it's working, but still no answer. "The boys really ah in trouble," Pimento says to himself. Tony never leaves his phone in the car. The young men are screwed blue. Either the Cuzzins are someplace Tony couldn't possibly use his phone, like a swimming pool or jacuzzi, or Meatballeyes is getting a forgettable handjob in the passenger seat. There's not much anyone can do about that.

Some time after Fiesta, a Cuz who attended the rave confesses to Pimento he never saw Tony's IROC. But he did see plenty of drunk Taus, the kinds of mountains of inebriated flesh men less courageous and more moral would have run from. "I sweah two of 'em wuh pawin' each utha," says an anonymous Cuz who agreed to be interviewed only after the author bought him a paint can for whippets. "It was like watchin' wild animals on those T.V. shows scratch themselves on trees and shit."

What happens next to the crew of the *IROC-Z* is anybody's guess. If the guys thought they were in trouble, they were experienced enough to get out of nearly any situation. But the Cuzzins could be so loopy they may *want* to dig their own graves. Fat chicks are like jury duty to undersexed studs—some kind of carnal self-inflicted wound that keeps ya honest every few years. With weirdos like Baloney and V.D., it's not hard to fathom. But by all estimations, the Cuzzins are rollicking with Taus, and dreading every minute of it. The Boulevard is hopping and the Fiesta's underway. The Cuzzins are nowhere to be found.

There's not much the crew can do but take their problem face first, like a ship into a tidal wave, and pray word never gets out. Machismo compounds the crew's woes. Someone could sweet-talk his way free or elude the Tau's grip and make a run for it. But facing your Cuzzins again after abandoning them is inevitable. The humiliation of being dropped from the circle may be worse than bedding a Tau. Besides, if one man leaves, another will have to endure two Taus—certain death. Although the chances of other Cuzzins carousing out of Gloucester on Fiesta

Eve are preposterous, it *could* happen. If Tony could call Pimento or Vermann for directions out of Hades, he'd have definitely done so by now. All he'd have to do to prevent word of tonight's disaster from spreading throughout the island is bribe the boys with beer and burgers, keep a calm, steady voice, and seem upbeat when asking about the girlie action back home. If Tony mentions car trouble, someone low on the Scrotum Pole will be sent to search and rescue. (Cuzzins left behind are expected to activate cellphones and pagers without hesitation.) A grease monkey and Camaro expert are beckoned to round out the crew. The remaining captains check trunks and garages for tools and replacement parts. Spare gas, oil, brake or transmission fluid, antifreeze, heck even windshield wash, is gathered, collected and readily accessible. Once Search and Rescue arrives, they stay, until the disabled vehicle is nursed to running again or safely towed to a Cuz-approved mechanic.

Presumably then, Tony's cellphone is off. No one receives a call. Tony's palm-sized cell is black and smooth, like the shell of a mussel. It has a "Caller ID" panel that warns the owner of pests. It also has a "Call Self" feature. With the discreet touch of a button, Tony can fake receiving an important call to get out of a jam. Between exes and parole advisors, Tony's learned to be stealthy when necessary. Cuzzins and Glochicks always complain of quiet social lives. To combat boredom, cells and pagers are constantly blipping and bleeping. When several calls go unanswered, the majority of the Boulevard is aware something unexpected may have happened. Tony's cell also has the ability to summon several numbers simultaneously (Multi-dialing) and leave prerecorded messages. It's only used when he breaks down. Multi-dialing is like hearing Mama scream across the fire escape to come for Sunday's spaghetti dinner. You drop what you do and go home. No questions asked.

That never happens. Tony must be confident his crew can endure. By now it's quite possible the Taus are in the "heavy petting" stage. The TV or radio is off, and the giant Taus are pawing and flipping their mates around like grits on a griddle. As each minute passes, the Cuzzins feel the pressure of all that flesh cascading and slapping around their bodies. Taus spasm so violently and without warning, a healthy man could snap in two. Tendons peel and hamstrings curl fast as snapped windowshades. It could be the same kind of violence that ruined Chinstrap Calzone. At some point, a Tau may get her hand under Johnny's buttonfly and onto Meester Joe, seriously screwing with their communicative abilities.

This is Johnny to Meester Joe. What you feel is nothing. Just pretend I'm doing yoga in my silk pajammies again. Come back.

This is Meester Joe. Sorry Johhny, I don't copy. I most certainly feel something. It's making me stronger than I've ever been. I think I'm growing. I feel like the Superman's angry dad! Over.

No Meester Joe! Must think non-erecting thoughts . . . Gay men dancing . . . Sailor boys swinging . . . Mall Santa sweating . . . Over.

Transmission fading . . . Size increasing . . . Only hearing pops and buzzes . . . Can't contain energy . . . Must build bookshelf! Must stop nuclear war!

Meester Joe, retreat! That's a direct order! Retreat!

I'm dancing Johnny! I'm dancing . . .

Meester Joe? Meester Joe, are you still there? Can you copy?

My God Johnny, everything's so dark and quiet in here. What is happening? Hey look at me! I'm ten feet tall!

Every Cuz reacts differently to sleeping with a large woman. A man once jeopardized his Cuzzinship by swearing in front of a roomful of Glochicks he's gay. He is forced to surrender his badge. The IROC-Z crew, all proud chauvinists, are probably shrugging this off as the low watermark of their lives. Just an off night. It could happen to anyone. At least they brought squids. As veterans, Tony and Meatballeyes must have their business faces on. Why panic? They'll need all the strength they can muster. And hey, you never know, perhaps the Taus feel too embarrassed to fool around in crowded company, right? Maybe not. "Legend has it Chinstrap's girl cornered him at the bottom of a salad bar," Pimento recollects. "She was shameless I tell ya. Shameless!"

Either way you look at it, the ugly truth must be one swift kick in the nuts for Baloney, Meatballeyes, Ditalini, Rigatoni, and Ziti. If they are in a hotel or dorm room somewhere, they've certainly been paired with partners as the Taus saw fit. Each has no idea if another crewman wants to run, or worse, stay. They went out as a crew and they'll go down as one too. Everything happening from this point forward is entirely up to the Taus.

This must be eating Johnny Ziti alive. His first big night outside Glosta and he hits the Feta Alpha Tau jackpot. If he had any backbone, he would have stayed in town with Yo-Yo Onenut howling at wet boobies. Afterwards, he'd be inside his grimy apartment, avoiding Goita like the plague and scraping resinators for Tina Cafeena. They'd split a pizza and talk about how Johnny was gonna win a Megadeth mirror for her at the carnival with one important dart toss. Instead, he selected Warehouse Door #1, and the psychological damage will last a helluva lot longer than a four-day Fiesta.

•

On their first date, Johnny and Tina attended the GHS Football Thanksgiving Game Pep Rally amongst dozens of friends. As the audience filed out the gymnasium, Cuzzins and Glochicks mulled around the bike racks in the parking lot, telling stories over a couple smokes. In a quiet moment, all eyes gazed upon one very distinct grouping. There was a burly man and saddlebagged woman, orbited by seven frenetic butterballs. It was the Calzones. Johnny was awestruck. Every Cuz had heard of Chinstrap Calzone: Man, Myth and Legend. And there he was, out for all to see. Out of respect, the gathering hushed. Chinstrap paused before the Cuzzins, looked back at his family—

and swallowed hard. Words were not necessary. Salutations would be awkward. What do you say to the man who lost it all?

Chinstrap wanted to make a fist. Instead he ambled into the night. From above, an lone acoustic guitar twinkled a lullaby across the autumn sky. A figure in the shadows hauntingly began to sing:

The Ballad of Chinstrap Calzone

Well there was a Cuz born at the Fort
Who outdid men in every sport
With confidence and style and grace supreme
Strong as cod, tall as a tuna
For years we cheered the Big Kahuna
Each Glostaman and Glostagirl's wet dream

Ol' Chinstrap Calzone! You never should have ever
　left your town
Ol' Chinstrap Calzone! One underhanded woman
　took you down

The buzz was one Cuz knew all the tricks
Our son could run, punt, pass and kick
And put ole Gloucester High back on the map
Big Ten men said He'd go so far
Our isle finally had a star
You should've seen the treasures in His lap

Ol' Chinstrap Calzone! You never should have ever
　left your town
Ol' Chinstrap Calzone! One evil-minded woman
　took you down

But in games of chasing girls and such
Chin got so dumb his ears could touch
No one would doubt He had more balls than brains
Each time Chin saw a girl's behind
His buttonfly's would lock and bind
Til one night when some gal screamed out His name

Well Ol' Calzone had hid His squids
In nine months time He had three kids
The news made every Cuzzin back home groan
The crown atop of Gloucester's king
Got yanked thanks to His ding-a-ling
So goes the tale of Ol' Chinstrap Calzone

Ol' Chinstrap Calzone! You never should have ever left your town
Ol' Chinstrap Calzone! One underhanded woman took you down

Ol' Chinstrap Calzone! Where was your head Cuz? Dang, you should've known
Ol' Chinstrap Calzone! You're gone forever Ol' Chinstrap Calzone

•

Growing up, everything Chinstrap touched turned to gold. Then, in one horrific transfer of bodily fluids, his life ended. If shit could happen to Chinstrap Calzone, shit could happen to anyone. That night after the pep rally, standing naked before a full-length bedroom mirror, Johnny Ziti promised Meester Joe that what happened to Chinstrap would never happen to them.

•

Now here he is—nothing more than a midnight snack. Heavy petting has ended, and Johnny is probably being dragged into some dirty corner of a private room like a caveman's dinner. "It's when they take you away from the others that the first waves of nudity begin," says Frankie Vermann. Johnny may be getting thrown onto a bare mattress on the floor: The lack of a bed frame provides the Tau with ample traction. That way nothing, except Johnny's lung capacity, can collapse. She may be above him, she may be below. In the frenzy, Johnny may catch a glimpse of another crewman getting tugged and uprooted to another room.

This may be the last chance for sensible contact between Johnny and Meester Joe.

Johnny to Meester Joe. Are you still with me?
Barely Johnny. Temperature increasing. All systems on standby.
Just stay still Meester Joe. Someone will find us. Can you sit tight for me?
I don't know about you Johnny, but Meester Joe's tight as a drum.
You must resist Meester Joe. Do you copy? Over.
Meester Joe don't work that way, Johnny. Meester Joe has only two functions: Catnap and Fertilize.
Sweet Mutha Mary!

Though no one's sure where the Taus may be entertaining the men of the IROC-Z, the Boulevard crews can easily assume the Tau chapterhouse. Many have been there, then ran like hell to get out. The house is gigantic, with three separate floors, spacious living rooms and full kitchenettes. Tumbling off these rooms are several bathrooms and bedrooms. Giant berry bushes surround the foundation, and have broken many a fall from mortified and revolted young men diving through windows for safety. Neighbors testify dozens of men run screaming from the estate each semester. The locals have a name for the FAT chapterhouse: Alcatraz.

It's not far-fetched to conjure visions of a younger Tony Baloney or Petey Meatballeyes plummeting through an open chapterhouse window, brushing leaves and grass clippings from his sweaty torso, tucking underwear like a football under his arm and stomping into the darkness of the long and winding driveway to the property's end, searching for the familiar shape of an IROC to return him to Gloucester.

Whatever it is, one thing's for sure. By daybreak Fiesta Thursday, something utterly big and beefy happens to the men of the IROC-Z.

•

If foreplay doesn't subside, the most Johnny can hope for is to stay awake until dawn. Then at least he'll have a chance at outlasting the Tau—now it's unthinkable. "In Tau carousals there is so much flesh above and below a man, that it becomes impossible to tell where one stomach stahts and anutha begins," says Vermann. In such conditions a temporarily free Cuz could never break away. So, for the next countless hours, the crew must keep their wits about them and pray they don't encounter an unexpected straddling. Hamhock thighs and double chins are roaming the bedsheets as if gushed from a geyser and there's not much Johnny can do but try to satisfy the beast before she mounts. If he were to be rolled over and momentarily bob above the bedspread, escape would not be an option—he'd just feel the giant shanks of flesh surround him and pull downward, over a hip, under a belly, and Meester Joe descending into a wet crevice too steep to survive.

•

"Five drunk Taus in my IROC—I'd shit sideways," says Bobby Zucci. "That's bigga than the pumpkin that won last year's

Topsfield Fair. I've driven some big girls around, I'm not ashamed to say, and my machine bucked like a muthafuggin' bronco. But that was just one girl at a time. *Five* Cuzzins and *five* Taus togetha? No way. You're dead. And then you're in *bed* with one! Holy Mackerel! Slap my ass and call me Angel. Wait—don't put that in the book."

When Bobby Zucci found himself rather surprisingly at the Feta Alpha Tau chapterhouse one evening during his heyday, his sexual encounter wasn't a tortuous marathon on a hardwood floor, but a desperate freestyle dash in a waterbed. Zucci was 18 at the time, old enough to hit a home run, they say, but too young to control his bat. A friend sneaked him into a college bar, and the two found themselves licking salt off their wrists and shooting pool with a pair of Taus. Bobby, the kind of guy who can't say no, couldn't refuse a midnight invitation from the older, bigger, brawnier Taus. Last call ended with another round of tequila, a wink and a nod, and then a nightcap at the chapterhouse. The atmosphere was casual and cordial. By dawn Bobby was bareass and battered.

"I was doin' fine. You aim your johnson under a bellybutton and grip for dear life—bounce your noggin off the headboard a hundred times and take it. You get the sweat out of your eyes when you can and hold your breath. There was a fair to moderate jiggle factor so I kept my eyes shut. I'd feel a splash every now and then and pray it was the bed burstin', I just couldn't tell.

It ended quick. We were movin' up and down almost vertically—I clearly rememba seein' the clock/radio on the shelf set at KISS 108. I rememba hearin' my buddy outside hollerin' for me to get out. She dug one of her heels into a lampshade, don't ask me how, and flipped me face-down. It was completely dark, and I heard her open a desk drawer lookin' for Crisco. She mumbled some and went to anutha desk at the otha side of the bed. I was flipped face-up.

As she rotated I saw a small tunnel of light beneath her. I didn't know if it was God or the Coast Guard. I couldn't see anything below my chest—I figured that was the easiest way to go. I slid feet-first, completely unda. It reminded me of when I was a troublemaker kid runnin' through the car wash. Then I was up—and I could sit up and breathe. I didn't look behind me. Neva got my clothes. Just found an open window and went for it."

Bobby Zucci still doesn't know how he sprung free. He simply sensed an escape route and slithered away. Whether Tony's crew is face-up or down, or bound and gagged and having their nipples tickled, they are in positions from which they cannot recover. Cuzzins call this The Devil's Ditch—the point of no return. The Taus are grinding and churning so dramatically there isn't time to blink. Magnets fly off refrigerators, headboards crack plaster, and oodles of meat thrash bedframes. In the frenzy, a man's eyes grow wide. He sees death for the first time. The experience is no longer sexual, it's survival. It's been said Cuzzins in extreme situations pray out loud in Italian, even if they never spoke it before. Every kid from the Boulevard is warned time and again the consequences of not finding a Keepah.

You can bet they're praying now. When clothes are stripped away, there's nothing but nakedness and terror. An avalanche of perspiration and flesh topple the stunned body. Virtually millions of surreal thoughts creep into the mind while lapsing in and out of consciousness. It may be the only time in a Cuz's life he feels shame—besides homoerotic hazing when trying out for Factory football. Wire bras burst open and the magnitude of freefalling breasts may remind someone of Old Glory herself, unfurling before a nor-east gale on Easter morn'. Muscles tighten and teeth clench; Sinatra croonings dance around the brain. Then it's time to latch onto anything, a bedpost, an end table, a palm tree, and brace for the storm. Under the skin is suffocating blackness. If the wind hasn't been knocked from you, it will rush out. Air will escape somewhere, perhaps under an armflap, across shaggy bellyhair, or through a pillowcase. When blood circulation is cut, the body goes numb. First the extremities, then torso, and finally a wispy lightheadedness. If you're lucky still, your mind will go blank as conscience suppresses the details.

The instinct for Cuzzins to chase what they perceive are highly attractive chicks is so strong that a sexual encounter with anything less than a Keepah stunts the fascination. No matter how repelled Johnny is, he doesn't give in to Meester Joe's requests until there is no alternative. He's erect, but not aroused. At that point Johnny's brain and body are riding on different rails. The wiring that feeds signals back and forth is disconnected. The majority of neurological activity has slid from the brain, down the central nervous system, and now resides below the belt. Meester Joe, for better or worse, is now at the helm. It's as if he's saying to Johnny, *I understand your confusion. It's nothing to be ashamed of or disgusted by. Because everything here is warm and dewy. And man, that's okay.* When the missile reaches the launch pad, so to speak, all non-sexual tubing is shut off. Meester Joe's mission is bluntly apparent. There is no possibility of a "pee break."

The incredulity of what is happening forces Johnny to think. It's the first time he and Meester Joe have had cheap sex and not enjoyed it. In situations like this, the two were always in control. Now *they're* being manipulated. "So this is what it was like for virgins on the jayvee rifle team," a doomed Cuz might think. "This is what it's for those strange and quiet foreign exchange students in math lab."

Doubling the Cuz's disbelief is guessing how life will continue afterwards. Recovery from such an experience may never occur. Aside from physical pain, mental anguish and humiliation should keep a Cuz from the Boulevard for years. For 30,000 people, Gloucester is awfully tight-knit. Gossip hits the hair salons, pizza joints and beaches in an instant. You carry a cloud, a scarlet letter, and every pill-popping, police-scanning housewife in the city knows your story.

Returning with your tail between your legs is known, and not affectionately, as the "Walk of Shame." Having never settled for the bottom of the barrel before, or the entire barrel for that matter, a defeated Cuz pouts and dodges his way through a barrage of catcalls and headslaps. It's a pitiful display. Reputations are forever tarnished. It's only then a Cuz learns what position he truly holds on the Scrotum Pole.

These thoughts ricochet through the mind when a Cuz finally gives in. Meester Joe can hold on just a little longer—any unexpected reach-around can trigger an external explosion. In any case, Meester Joe is getting stronger and plumper. He's become a "routney," the hardest form of an erection prior to ejaculation. The clock is running down now. Johnny's too weak to think of not impregnating the Tau. He's already resigned to imagining his life some years from now, his tenth year high school reunion perhaps, with eight kids hanging around him like seagulls to a trawler.

Occasionally someone survives the routney stage. It is from these people that we know what fat sex feels like. In 1892, the son of an Lanesville pastor named Miko Spatula was on a church social bound for Old Salem when they ran into a group of wood nymphs (hysterically repressed Protestants) in the dead of night. More than 30 parishioners were escorted against their will to nearby villages, tethered, and coaxed into manhood. But Spatula managed to fight his way from under a damp blanket and into an air pocket. Alas, the nymph's grip tightened, dragging him down, and the last thing he remembers is leaving a trail of fingernail marks on the straw floor. A few minutes later the buoyancy of the Holy Spirit, Miko swears, spit him back into the safety of the forest, and he lived to write about his experiences in the *Gloucester Daily Times*. It's as close as one is going to get to the last untarnished moments of the *IROC-Z* crew's sex life. Unfortunately, Spatula's article wasn't printed near the *Times*' obituaries or police notes. So until now, no one has read it.

All evening the monsters converged on our party as we felt our way through the wood paths, whilst nightfall came only to add darkness to our horrors. Shortly before 10 o'clock the nymphs penetrated our parade, carrying each of us into the blackness, and our situation was desperate. The end came quickly thereafter, when an undergarment of sorts was positioned into my mouth, and my body trudged through the thickets and hucklebrush. With scarcely time to think I fastened the buckles of my trousers and, joining the others in the Act of Contrition, pressed the Saint Christopher to my bosom. There was no time to spare to study humanity at this juncture, but I can never forget the lack of struggle in all I passed. My companions seemed paralyzed, some lifelong holy men. The eldest of the group, uttering cries of despair and last farewells, seemed frozen in time—as if waiting for their sinning body parts to drop to the ground before them and burst into flame. It was by sheer erotic curiosity that I was able to ignore them. Once indoors, a perfect mountain of flesh seemed to come from overhead, as well as from below, and dashed me against the stovepipe. The animal was ready to bed, and I was pulled down with it, struggling to extricate myself.

I was put on all fours, got my wrists held above me, as if on the rack, and immediately wriggled my heels, only to further entrench myself. This exertion was a serious waste of breath, and after ten or fifteen seconds the effort of ejaculation could no longer be restrained. Many years ago my pastor used to describe how painless and easy the ultimate sin was—"like voices melting in a choir"—and this flashed across my brain at the time. The "thrusting" efforts became less frequent, and the pressure seemed unbearable, but gradually the pain seemed to ease. I appeared to be in a pleasant dream, although I had enough will power to think of friends and the sight of the secluded quarries, familiar to me as a boy where my pastor would take me, that was brought to my view. Before losing consciousness the chest pain had completely disappeared and the sensation was actually heavenly—though not fit to eventually bear child, one would believe.

Upon finally awaking, I found myself at the surface, and managed to get a dozen good deep breaths. My britches were forty yards distant, and I used oil from a lamp to slip from the brute's grasp. On the path home, sound sleep set in, and this sleep lasted hours, when a profuse nausea came on, evidently brought on by whatever was ingested. Until sunrise crept overhead all my muscles were in a constant tremor which could not be controlled. Several weeks later I was in bed, curled in fetal comfort, and, late in the evening, began twitching as if summer corn roasting on open flame. Constables were summoned and struggled severely to control my spasms. In time, furious slapping settled my body, leading to unshakable grief.

Curcuru guesses Spatula's closet homosexuality and bondage fetish allowed him to survive the ordeal. The *IROC-Z* crew doesn't have that luxury. They are—unequivocally—straight and ignorant. Not one last repulsive thought—say a shirtless hobo licking his mustache and rubbing his zipper—can save them now. At some point, the guys can expect the Taus' hips to lock, see the eyes of the beast, stare into the mouths of hell, and realize all is lost. Their genitalia, having imposed increasingly drastic measures to dissuade the pleasurable sensations, have finally given in. The vas deferens, the reproductive tubing responsible for cannoning life's recipe for babies from one idiot to the next, is ready to release. The gonads, (Johnny Ziti refers to his as the Wondertwins), prepare for detonation. They throb dully—"like a hangover headache," as one Cuz says. The Wondertwins continue to throb until, after one last push, they are empty. It's up to the vas deferens now.

The Cuzzin does not know what has happened to his body; all he knows is he's about to release a seed. Orders are still being issued—*Turtle! Wrinkle! Retreat!*—that the Meester Joes cannot obey. The body is doing everything it can to delay the inescapable.

The hamster wheel inside the heads of five young men who left Gloucester dredges to a halt as soon as they are mounted, whether on a couch, waterbed, or, God help us all, the rear of a beautiful 1987 ocean-blue IROC-Z Camaro. The mind sloshes like quicksand, a place where thoughts and dreams are perverted with each bloodcurdling lunge. The only way to avoid serious trauma at this point would be to pass out or will oneself to a vegetative state.

Climax finally arrives, and the results are inevitably gruesome. When everything is said and done, all the blood, all the sensations, all transferable liquids arrive at the epicenter of a Cuz's world: his groin. Sweat beads around temples, knees weaken and buckle, lungs grip one last breath until . . . the nightmare ends. Meester Joe recoils and, not unlike a flood victim, quickly gathers his belongings and heads for high ground.

The limp bodies of the five young men could be likened to the fiberglass carcasses of yesteryear's sports cars lining the junkyard near Tony Baloney's childhood home. The paint has lost its sheen and the engine is shot. They may, by some miracle, run again one day, but never like they used to. Baloney, Meatballeyes, Rigatoni, Ditalini, and Ziti are laid.

8

Unskinny Bop

Lorenzo Pimento:

*I*t wasn't until afta I talked to Tony last that I knew how much trouble they was in. Guys from Poppycock Cove I know said the rave was a huge send-off for graduatin' Taus. I shit myself. My crew tries avoidin' Tau pahties because you know what's gonna happen. We just stay home and play video games. And they throw pahties in the middle of the woods and shit. It's bad enough you're outta Glosta, but imagine gettin' lost in Poppycock, or Boston?

My friend said there was lots of Xtasy goin' on, and that shit's like Spanish Fly to Taus. His friends wouldn't even go in the warehouse. They stayed in the cah and split an eighth. Everyone who went there said it was the most Taus they'd eva seen. You could tell there was old Taus there and freshmen recruits. It must've looked like a meat locka. You can go to a million pahties and there's always some fatties. But imagine if that's all there was was fatties? That could break a man.

Some guys said the women's rugby team showed up. That's another ton. If those guys showed up wantin' to get laid and ran into that, they'd get fuggin' whooped. I only talked to a few people who were there. They looked like they just got back from latrine duty. I was lucky. I'm seeing a sixth-grader with a 10:30 curfew. I had to stay in town that night.

•

Despite the news, or lack thereof coming from the other side of the Bridge, Pimento is having quite an evening to remember. His new girlfriend had been tucked in bed before the successful get-together with Vermann's gang at Wingaersheek. In the early morning hours he arrives at the Boulevard with a full wallet, having collected three phone numbers and a dimebag. The Cadillac *Seville 1* celebrates the first morning of Fiesta with a little "pahk and spahk" as the sun speckles the Harbor. The combination of potent THC, a sleepless night, and the dreamlike excitement of Fiesta morning momentarily pacify Pimento's crewmen. Between giggles and chills they playfully dream of happy endings for their missing brethren.

Maybe someone jumped out the bathroom window. Maybe Tony kept the car running. Did everyone find a Tau? Did everybody stay?

Unfortunately the positivity, like the pot, is only temporary.

Presumably, the *IROC-Z* will not be back Fiesta Thursday to hog a parking space near the Man-at-the-Wheel. That will be the air raid siren heard 'round the Harbor. The dough's in the fryalator and Tony ain't in town. No Camaro means mayday.

9

Tina Cafeena Talks

"Of course I knew there was a problem, that Camaro's always on the Boulevahd," says Tina Cafeena, Johnny Ziti's girlfriend. "I had some 5-4's and dreamt this wickit kweah dream. I sleepwalked out the apahtment and see a wiggid yellow IROC pahked by the Statue. I can see two people foolin' around in there. I know it's Johnny. I don't know why, because I can't see him, but I know. I try openin' doors screamin', Johnny! Johnny! He just keeps on sexin'. So I use my class ring to break a window. I try to get a grip but everything's oily and greasy and I'm losing my mind at Johnny and then I see his football jacket. I grab it and look for my cheerleadin' pin but I know it's gone. Then I wake up and look ova old scratch tickets fuh winnaz."

It's the morning of Fiesta Friday. No one's heard from the *IROC-Z* since Air Guitar Night. The town is so crazy, few in Glosta realize some of their own are missing. Tina Cafeena matches lemons and cherries on lotto tix while the 5-4's wear off, then walks around the driveway overlooking the Greasy Pole and its platform. Party boats fill the Harbor. A bright orange flag waves and waits at the end of a pole for that day's champion. No one has spoken to Tina, and she has heard nothing on Goita's police scanner. She smacks a giant wad of watermelon bubblegum, watching the Cut go up and down, up and down. Suddenly, Tulip appears.

Tulip is Tony's mom. It was her boyfriend, Bobby Zucci, who introduced her son to his first Camaro. She lives out of state now, but revisits every year for Fiesta. Bobby told Tulip the *IROC-Z* hadn't come in. In a trance, Tulip walked the Boulevard, wishing she'd find Tony and the gang. When she didn't, she made the painful trek across the street to Goita's.

Tina can tell Tulip doesn't want to see her.

"Tina, honey," says Tulip, "I think you're the last to know. The boys got stuck in Boston. Tony's friends can't raise him on the pager."

Tina tries blocking frightful thoughts by reciting aloud chalkboard specials at the clamshack. "Fisherman Platter: includes scallops and fish cheeks, $11.95. Sautéed fresh mussels in white sauce, served over linguine, $9.95. Broiled fresh scrod topped with seasoned crumbs, $12.95." She's still on 5-4's, still grabbing Johnny's jacket, and Tulip's pitying eyes tell Tina the ugly truth. Johnny's sexin'. Johnny's gone and done bad.

Tulip says there's a good chance Tony has no clue how to work a pager, but a Glochick knows better. Tina runs down the Boulevard between the beach and Statue. It's seven in the morning, the drooling and senile have completely saturated both sides of Western Ave. Some Cuzzins are there too, teetering and scramble-eyed. Yo-Yo OneNut is there. So are Frankie Vermann and his crew. The rumors are out and no one knows for sure— but some Cuzzins liquoring up for the Pole assume the worst.

Tina starts pounding wine coolers. "People were playin' stupid because they knew I'd go apeshit," she says. "And it's hard to tell who knew and who didn't because they're all dumba than a sack of bananas anyway. They weren't on the scanna or in the police notes. Johnny's got my varsity pin. He even paid for this stupid engagement ring tattoo. Now he's gone. I can just pitcha it too: Johnny and Petey and Vito hangin' 'round some drunk hoochies, probably stupid and fat and ugly. And they pretend they got awesome jobs and cahs and no girlfriends. I know, that's how Johnny met me. And I bet they were eggin' each utha on, completely forgettin' about us back here. Then they split and go their own ways. But did he think of me when he was with that girl? She's probably wickit kweah anyway."

Bobby Zucci isn't at the Boulevard—and with his track record of selling duds—he sure isn't welcome. He's in a phone booth, scanning a directory of North Shore Camaro dealers and mechanics. He's been trying to learn if anyone has seen or heard from a gorgeous ocean-blue model. He's also tried talking to Frankie Vermann and Lorenzo Pimento, but they are too far into their Fiesta weekends. Zucci drives to a mandatory meeting of business leaders in the city. As a bouncer at one of the shadiest bars during Fiesta, Zucci must learn to keep a straight face when asking for $10 cover charges. But he can't get his mind off his old Camaro. He leaves the meeting early.

Back in the phone booth, Zucci finally finds Lorenzo Pimento. "They were supposed to check Vito in for the Pole already," Pimento says. "Now I think he's off the competitor's list."

"That cah needs to be back where it belongs," Zucci cries. "Back in Glosta!"

At five o'clock, only minutes before the start of the Greasy Pole, Zucci tries one last time to raise the *IROC-Z*. Nothing. Pimento can't raise her either. It's been two days since Tony Baloney was heard from. Zucci walks the length of Pavilion Beach to the Man-at-the-Wheel alerting the fleet.

Meanwhile, gossip queens have picked up and run with the story. A cloud of half-truths and innuendo seep into the summer's haze. Before the day's first drunk and disorderly arrest, word is a blue IROC *and* Lorenzo Pimento's Bigfoot *America* are missing. The hair salons are overwhelmed with gabbing girls. Before you know it, every Cuz's girlfriend knows what happened to Tina Cafeena. "Once a Cuz goes ova the Bridge his guy friends forget him," explains OneNut's ex. "But us girls they leave behind can't.

We're addicts. We're like parasites with no hosts or suntin'. I just learned that on Animal Planet."

The fact of the matter is the rest of Gloucester's finest are having a great Fiesta. The weather is perfect for bikinis and beer. OneNut considers sailing outside the Harbor on a buddy's boat for an expedition to Poppycock Cove to see if the guys are marooned. He tried reaching them after the Air Guitar competition and again Fiesta Thursday. By Friday, OneNut figures they're racing back for the Pole, an event they couldn't miss. He tells Lorenzo Pimento something must have gone wrong. Pimento passed that thought a day back. All senior Cuzzins agree to meet in the parking lot across the downtown Dunkin' Donuts to swap info. Cuzzins believe their girls know nothing about the secretive nightlife off the island. Their opinions are not pertinent. It'll be up to Glosta's remaining studs to calculate how five of their own, even if they *were* out of their minds, could miss Fiesta. Another IROC captain suggests a dealership off Route 1 as a place where broken-down dream machines often convalesce. "There aren't many places a Cuz can trust to bring his vehicle," says OneNut. "We know the dudes that buy 'em, sell 'em, and work on 'em. If we can't find the *IROC-Z*, I figya they're way outta Boston or got in some real fuggin' pigshit."

Some Cuzzins at the meeting note Tony never keeps his pager on or answers phone calls when he's with a woman. OneNut phones his buddy with the boat: No sign of the guys in the Harbor or on the Greasy Pole platform. But someone says he hears two clicks, a snort and a giggle on Tony's line, though he can't regain further contact. Someone else thinks Vito is on the Pole platform in a wedding gown, but after a Jello shot pops off the suspect's head to grab his attention, it proves to be untrue. Every Cuz with $200 shades and a cellphone tries calling the *IROC-Z*. Tony and the boys have fallen off the edge of the island.

The rest of the force at Dunkin' Donuts tries to determine exactly who is aboard Tony's Camaro. Joe Tomatoes doesn't know—he's about as sharp as a carp anyway—and a Cuz who parks in Tony's usual spot assumes the crew left for fishing. Finally, some scab says he's talked to Mad Dog, a Vermann crewman who saw the guys in Boston the night they disappeared. He lists everyone he noticed waiting in line for zazeets: Tony Baloney, Sal Rigatoni, Vito Ditalini and Petey Meatballeyes. Mad Dog says the other guy's a rookie, someone he'd seen at the tanning salon in the past. "I skipped Air Guitah for the first time eva," says Mad Dog. "I figured if there was any night to miss, it would be Wednesday. But Boston sucked so I came back. From the looks of 'em in the Camaro, you could tell none of 'em was gettin' any. If they did, they must've got some real skanks."

The night the *IROC-Z* departed, Pimento told Yo-Yo OneNut Cuzzins were heading to Boston, in case he was interested. OneNut ran to Goita's with Cuz-in-training Joe Tomatoes. When he saw four jittery men planning to leave, he balked, and settled for wet T-shirts and air guitars instead. That's when Meatballeyes appeared and dealt himself in as shotgunner. Next thing Yo-Yo remembers, Meatballeyes is in the passenger seat. The *IROC-Z* left with five Cuzzins and a cooler. All Yo-Yo OneNut knows now is he's at the Greasy Pole and those guys aren't.

10

St. Peter's Fiasco

By the time word spreads throughout Glosta that Tony's crew isn't back from Boston, the drunken revelry of Fiesta weekend is in high gear. Rivers of cars and humanity clog every inlet to and outlet from the city. In all, Gloucester's population is more than doubled during the long weekend. The heart of the action, the carnival and bar scene, takes place in the West End. That's roughly somewhere between the Man-at-the-Wheel and Gloucester's most famous yuppie bar, the Crow's Nest. It's there the masses customarily spill onto Pavilion Beach for a bird's eye view of the Greasy Pole.

So voluminous is the crowd, for once the local police department may be justified working so many road detail hours. Besides, each year brings a new slew of rumors of possible drive-bys, stakeouts and coke busts to keep everyone interested. This year's rumor is that a bunch of kids from Lawrence, after a run-in with boisterous Gloucester supporters during the last cheerleading competition, may want to raise some hell at Stage Fort Park. For those unfamiliar with the area, Stage Fort Park, a public picnic ground around the corner from the Man-at-the-Wheel, is apparently the only public park between Spanish Harlem and Cuba.

On Sunday, the last day of Fiesta, the day of the weekend's

grand finale, (an overhyped fireworks display), Gloucester's Cuzzes mindlessly follow a familiar pattern of party-crashing and prepping for the champion's Pole. The sights, sounds and smells are the same, but the void left by the *IROC-Z* and five missing crew wallows in everyone's mind: Three days and four nights of Fiesta, and no clues to their whereabouts.

More stories begin to surface about what may have happened in the warehouse Fiesta Eve. An ironworker from Lynn claims to have been overpowered by a Tau: His air mattress popped like a cork. Extraordinary reports of neck and back injuries are reported in hospitals in Danvers and Salem. A local pony jockey is hugged by a Tau and not seen for days. One sorry bastard, in a moment of desperation, is cajoled to join a Tau for her homecoming. Over one hundred egos are bruised in the town of Poppycock Cove alone. One makeshift bartender that evening is no longer able to speak. All he does is pull his hair out in clumps, lick it, and stick it in a desk drawer.

The sorority unleashes such a wave of terror, panicky drivers inundate Poppycock Cove's byways for hours trying to escape. The *IROC-Z* may have been a spec in that surf. But there are no witnesses. Had the rave taken place during a full chapter party, in which Tau's from across New England would gather in a boozy show of sisterhood, there might be an entire generation effected, not unlike Chernobyl. Nerds and virgins are cheered to see so many bullies forever psychologically impaired. Damage across the North Shore effects over a thousand virile men, Cuzzins and college guys alike.

"Put it this way," says Bobby Zucci. "At most sorority pahties one or two guys get swallowed. They're sayin' ten guys might be *engaged*. If that's true, it's the worst fuggin' disasta I've eva heard of. Youz guys'll neva see that again."

●

While many in Gloucester fiddle with the scant facts of the *IROC-Z*'s Fiesta Eve, a more concentrated effort is being formed at the Boulevard to conduct a search for the crew. Ten IROCs prepare to make the move southward over the Bridge after the fireworks. There's a half-baked rumor circulating that Tony Baloney called for Sunday's Pole odds, a rumor quickly dismissed. Guys like Frankie Vermann and Lorenzo Pimento plan on the unthinkable: leaving the island during Fiesta Sunday. Most of the caravan will be homesick by Exit 15. Truth be told: Many will turn around.

Nothing is seen or heard from the *IROC-Z* until the morning after Fiesta Sunday when Lorenzo Pimento, after a long night of searching, happens upon the warehouse in Poppycock Cove and finds a cooler in the woods. It's ten yards or so from the driveway and has "Outlaw" written on its lid in thick black marker. It's Tony's. "Looked like someone threw it around," Pimento recalls. "Just a few empty cans, that's all that was left."

Pimento also finds a comb, an empty dimebag, and a puked-upon tanktop. They don't necessarily belong to anyone from the *IROC-Z*, they could have come from any stud, but it's not a good sign.

Days later, when Vermann becomes comfortable enough to guess the Taus have left their sorority house for summer, he ventures there and makes several grave discoveries. A broken cigar and a gold chain with a barracuda pendant are lying under a window along with Tony's cellphone. The phone is in perfect working order, but its battery is gone. It may have been a desperate attempt from Tony to conceal his identity, or to keep his misadventures from the Boulevard. Normally, a Cuz never misplaces his phone. It's right next to his wallet, squids and varied female fake ID's.

Finally, during the Horribles Parade the following July 4th weekend, the virtual end of summer in Gloucester, a Tau is reportedly seen wearing the St. Peter's pin Tony kept on his dashboard. That pin is akin to an airliner's black box.

The probability of Tony discharging the pin is nonexistent. Even with the amount of girth in the car that evening taken into account, there is no way *anyone* but a Cuz would be allowed to lay a finger on the dashboard. No one who knows Tony can explain it. Not his mother Tulip, not Tulip's boyfriend Bobby.

•

The following autumn at the first big Feta Alpha Tau bash, an Essex man vows he sees one of the lost men, until he is whisked away before being fully recognized. From his Newell Stadium bleacher seat during the Gloucester High Thanksgiving Day football game, Lorenzo Pimento thinks he sees Tony's Camaro going over the Cut. Wrong again. By the end of Thanksgiving weekend, questions concerning the five missing Cuzzins subside. People have searched dozens of bars and clubs and beaches and bashes without a trace of the *IROC-Z*. All they have is a gold-plated fish with a diamond eye.

•

"I went to the Bridge a lot afta Fiesta," says Tina Cafeena. "Not all the way ova, just one side. I tried pitcharin' what the guys were goin' through when they passed every exit. Then the rave. I still don't believe that part. Johnny would neva creep with anutha girl again. Sometimes, I dream he'll come back and ask me to marry him on one of those casino cruises. I miss him a wickit lot. I'll see him someday. He don't do so good away from his mutha."

A symbolic kegger is held after the Thanksgiving Day game at Swinson's Field in East Gloucester. It's the first party at the popular ball field since teens were caught burning patio furniture along the third base line a few years back. Tony and Meatballeyes made the place famous by firing off M-80's and outrunning cops through the woods. Now people from long forgotten study halls and pep rallies who didn't know the lost Cuzzins are buying five-dollar keg cups. An inebriated Frankie Vermann, in an impromptu toast, warns the younger crowd of what evil lies beyond the Bridge, then crushes a can on his forehead.

OneNut and Tomatoes spin moped donuts on the infield. Lorenzo Pimento drinks an honorary funnel. Several youngsters vomit what appears to be fully formed Beef-a-roni. Everybody shuttles back and forth from the Boulevard to the ball field all night long.

•

If the ill-fated crew of the *IROC-Z* had simply gotten laid, the people of Gloucester could have had some sense of closure. But they didn't get laid. They got smothered and sullied and vanished from the Boulevard altogether. Even if they moved away or, gulp, fell in love, it would take a lot of St. Peter's pin-rubbing to wish them back. But life goes on. And the predatory night creatures of Glosta have very short memories. Others left on the island see the missing Cuzzins' girlfriends the way seagulls see chum. Opportunity.

"The night before the guys left for Boston I made plans for Vito and me," says Ditalini's underage girlfriend Velveeta. "We were gonna get pitchaz taken at the gazebo at Stage Fort. Then we was gonna get more pitchaz done in a real studio. Like us layin' on a carpet with a puppy and a balloon. But Vito didn't want to do it. He thought it was too gay. He threatened to drop me off in Rocky Neck and drive away without me. Next thing I know, it's Fiesta and Tina says Johnny hasn't come home. Vito's the love of my life, the centa of my universe, but most importantly, he's my buyah."

The first thing Velveeta does after speaking with Tina is buy three fried doughs. Then she calls Vito's parents to see if he's still on the list for Friday's Greasy Pole. Vito's dad is a fishermen, all the qualification Vito needed to make a weekend chase for the flag. Once Vito's parents answer Velveeta the only way they know how, in unintelligible Italian, she calls Bobby Zucci to see if he's found his old car. Zucci says that the car is unaccounted for and some Cuzzins are organizing an investigation around Sunday's fireworks. It appears Vito is going to miss the entire Fiesta. Velveeta and her friends wouldn't have anyone to buy liquor for four whole days. When she finally explains to her friends that Vito isn't coming back, they demand answers.

"Um, he's gettin' stuff from outta town," Velveeta says. "Yeah, he's gettin' fyaworks in New Hampsha."

Her friends know Vito constantly lights off fireworks, especially at Plum Cove Beach in Lanesville. "New Hampsha must be some place where they don't tax booze or cigarettes or fyaworks," they think unitedly. "We should totally fu'in move there."

Vito is the only adult of age the girls have to buy booze. After enduring Fiesta without hard lemonade and nips of Captain Morgan's, Velveeta's friends apparently become delusional while shoulder-tapping in front of their favorite packy.

On the night of July 4th, the girls claim they had just pulled into the parking lot and were waiting patiently, when from nowhere Vito appeared by the driver-side window. Before Velveeta's stupefied friends speak, Vito knowingly points to a peppermint schnapps ad on the front door. He walks into the store, but never walks out.

More people get spooked. Vito's father looks out his kitchen window one night and swears his son is practicing for Fiesta on a homemade greasy pole constructed in the backyard. In his boxers and T-shirt, he runs outside to cheer Vito on. But the image of his boy vanishes. And the pole: Not one ounce of grease.

Back at the apartment, Tina Cafeena has illusions of her own. She sees Johnny pull over in a brand new shadow-black 1LE IROC-Z. "Gotta find a tap," he says before she has a chance to answer. "Keg at Wingaersheek." Then he speeds off. "Johnny'd neva cheat on me," says Tina in hollow denial. "Even if he did, I'd find the skank and pull her hair out by the fu'in roots."

Tina does have doubts about her boyfriend, though. Sometimes she walks to the Boulevard and waits for Johnny to park by the Statue. But then she sees how other Cuzzins operate. (The girls of the other missing crewmen moved on to other, more muscley things.) Maybe Johnny *did* find someone else.

In time, she bounces around from new boyfriend to new boyfriend, but can't get used to wearing someone else's jacket. The *IROC-Z* never does return, nor any of Tony's crew. Having trouble facing reality, Tina believes the guys may have gone on a *really* long road trip. "Maybe they're teachin' tribes in Africa what the Greasy Pole is," she thinks. "It could happen. They do it in the movies all the time."

•

When it's understood Bobby Zucci's old car is lost forever, several rounds of beer-buying and apologizing doesn't restore his image. Fair or not, Zucci is seen as a careless owner and is forced to swear off Camaros altogether. He can forget about romancing any Glochick downtown for awhile, too, with the exception of Tulip.

When Johnny Ziti's unpaid apartment lease expires there is little leeway for Goita. Tina mooched there but can't be held responsible. And Goita wouldn't want to turn it into a legal battle on account of infinite building code violations. The only compensation she receives is a hundred bucks worth of *Senseless: Cologne for Men* and ten video games featuring topless skateboarding ninja robots.

Weeks pass before Yo-Yo OneNut rejoins the Boulevard fleet. He still counts his blessings about deciding to stay in town. When he heard Tony's crew was lost, he got engaged as fast as possible, making sure he anchored in Gloucester forever. Wedding plans keep Yo-Yo from the nightlife nowadays.

Vito Ditalini's father happily invites Yo-Yo to practice on the pole in his backyard so he can compete next Fiesta in Vito's name. Another anchor to keep a good Cuz grounded. It's the least OneNut can do for the Ditalinis. If *he* left Gloucester Fiesta Eve, it would have been *him* caught in a bear hug, pleading for his life, wishing he weren't so damn irresistible.

11

Me Cuzzin. Me No Understand

The following year, on Wednesday, Fiesta Eve, a stunning ocean-blue IROC-Z Camaro pulls in front of the Man-at-the-Wheel. Memories rush forth. Every single person at the Boulevard freezes. Tina Cafeena loses feeling in her legs. Goita storms from her apartment driveway and raps on the tinted windows. "I know you're in there, Ziti," she shouts. "I'd know this cah anywhere!"

The window slowly slides downward. Behind the wheel sits a man with slicked-back hair, skin-tight jeans, two pounds of gold chains and mirrored shades. This is *exactly* how people remember the crew leaving a year ago. The driver steps out ever so calmly, touching a Marlboro to his lips.

"Well I'll be damned," exhales Goita.

The man is not Johnny, or Tony, or Rigga, or Vito, or Meatballeyes. It's the new Joe Tomatoes. If Joe were really Italian, he'd yelp *"Gee fi!"* and dole out high-fives. People outside Gloucester may have a hard time believing a dirty white boy like Tomatoes, someone seriously lacking Mediterranean or Iberian ethnicity, can be so openly accepted as a Cuz. Nowadays however, anyone regardless of ethnic background or family fishing history can participate in the Greasy Pole on Fiesta Friday. (Meatballeyes was considered a Cuz and he was whiter than Wonderbread.) So the traditionalist community has come to terms with the inevitable meshing of cultures.

Now Tomatoes, like so many others, has climbed to the top of the Scrotum Pole. He is truly a Cuz. He has made the leap from pretender to contender with one simple move: The man bought himself an IROC. He captains his own crew now too. It's been one full year since Joe Tomatoes talked Yo-Yo OneNut out of a trip in Tony's Camaro. Joe admitted feeling uneasy about friends leaving the island, especially with the unpredictability of Fiesta hours away. He felt like a yellowbelly then but hid his true feelings like a good apprentice-Cuzzin should. Some guys can cut the cord. Joe Tomatoes wasn't ready—until now.

And then there are the truly uninitiated. Guys inside Tomatoes's IROC have literally never gone grocery shopping outside Gloucester. Anyone who grows up in this city quickly learns what it takes to be a Cuz. And being a Cuz lasts interminably longer than summer school or car payment plans. As time passes, the branches of Gloucester's family tree twist and tangle. In this daffy seaport, most Cuzzins *are* blood-related cousins. Each new generation of muscle and baby oil flexes the shore here as endlessly as the tide.

•

Fiesta Eve this time around is more insane than last year. As popularity of the Greasy Pole grows, so do the masses. Word is Old Timer's is forced to stop letting people in for the Air Guitar and Wet T-shirt Contest *by five o'clock*. But the promise of promiscuity overwhelms one ambitious Cuz. Joe Tomatoes is worried about female prospecting in the local bars. All fingers point to a night of sword fightin' and steak swingin'. He'll have to find treasure outside town. Joe gets a tip about a great new bar in Salem, a city historic for burning weird, white people. Salem is a crazy town, bigger than Gloucester. Thing is, Salem's bread and butter is Halloween, not the last long weekend in June. But there's no stopping Tomatoes's maiden voyage. If he's nervous, he's not showing it. He won't, even if his girlfriend Perri Oxide can't bring herself to letting go of Joe's belt ring. "Are you sure you wanna leave Glosta?" Perri asks. "We can ride the Zippa."

"We'll go tomorrow," he promises, looking his crew over. "This'll be good for us. It's OneNut's twenty-first. We're gettin' him fuggin' loaded."

That afternoon, Tomatoes and his boys celebrate OneNut's birthday by crawling him through every bar in the city for a shot. They chew pills and discuss Bob Marley's poetry. Someday, they promise each other, they'd open a bar, because that would be awesome. And give away lots of shots. That would be more awesome.

Their voyage down 128 goes as smooth as can be. Tomatoes does a very professional job behind the wheel. It's taken a lot to get to this point in his cruising career. He's had his hair braided and in dreadlocks, had friends stick needles in his ass to bulk him up, he's even been slapped with a couple restraining orders. Only now though has Joe Tomatoes finally realized his stud potential. Now, *he* has an IROC and a five-gallon drum of aftershave.

By midnight, the crew in Tomatoes's Camaro realize they won't return in time to make last call in Gloucester. Their attention turns to after-hours in Salem. What the Cuzzins don't know is that at some point during the night, in a club, on a dance floor, or in the passing lane, someone released an inadvertent signal, and from that moment forward a group of tipsy coeds have had their eyes on five unsuspecting hardbodies.

•

Four days later, a tow truck quietly drags a disabled blue IROC over the railroad tracks to the junkyard. An empty cooler lies yawning in the backseat. The driver promises he doesn't know whose vehicle it is. He's just following orders to bring it home for proper burial.

Tomatoes and his crew haven't been heard from since leaving. A burly, bronze gearhead searches the car for clues. He finds a handful of squids on the dash. The wrappers are empty. The Cuzzins in Joe Tomatoes's Camaro have been Tau'd.

**REWIND
REPEAT**

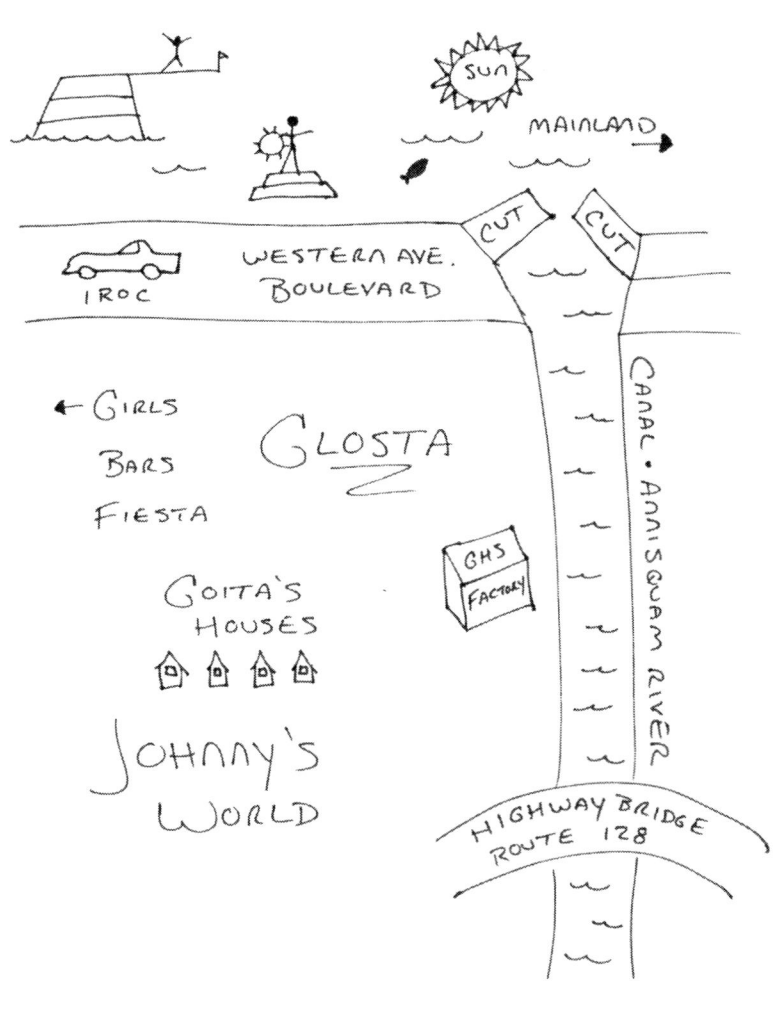

POST SCRIPT

Dear Ma and Pa,

    I am feeling rather lonesome today, so I thought I would commence a novel of our fair port city to pass away the time. I apologize for letting months pass between correspondence. I have been stranded in traffic behind the Cut Bridge on the Gloucester side of Western Avenue for what seems an eternity.
    Perhaps you would like to know how we refugees idle our time away? Well, each morning I tend to the seagull farm I started from scratch in the passenger seat. I clip them free of six-pack wrappers and feed them the gunk off the engine. They eat anything. Then I start the car up and let the engine run, all the while waiting for some neighbor or deputy man to point out the sign encouraging me to not damage the ozone. I use the back of a driver's manual to keep notes for my stories while listening to the only thing any radio around here can receive—that dang monotonous computerized marine forecast. Then I mischievously inch the car forward and back, preventing anyone with New York plates parked to my left from cutting in front of me.
    On a good day, I'll count whale watch boat after whale watch boat in hopes the last will travel through, and the Cut will finally descend. But it never happens. I can only pray we soon advance to the other side, for rations will subside, and sadly, I drank the last of the fresh radiator coolant days ago.

I am happy to report that G.G. and Lucy, the couple occupying the Pontiac behind me, have recently married and started a family. I've since grown close to their four children. Some days I let them and the dog run around the hood of my car.

I am nearly well of my lameness and my health is good. The rhubarb I've grown in the trunk ripened early this year, and along with the Slush Puppies from the nearby convenience mart, I am becoming fleshy again.

I am very thankful for the money, letters, and gasoline you sent me. I pray that traffic will lighten and my life be spared to repay the many kindnesses I have received.

Unfortunately, not all news from the Gloucester side of Western Avenue is cheerful.

I must regrettably report that Mr. Pennington, he of the Chevrolet Penningtons, passed away last winter. Since my heater was no longer in working order, G.G. and I decided it best to keep Mr. Pennington from spoiling by resting him in my car 'til the ground thawed.

The widow Pennington is a regular visitor now. She says she heard the gate to the Cut is jammed like brown sugar in a sweet potato pie—that the gate will never open and the bridge will never be passable again! She is such a gossip, Mother! Forgive me for saying, but you and Aunt Petunia couldn't hold a candle to ol' Mrs. Pennington's chitchatting!

I am happy to hear all is well on the Magnolia side on the mainland. How I long for the endless soccer fields. Please send your thoughts and two more quarts of 1030 when you are fit and able.

There is considerable excitement here, for word from the front is that the tourism season is close to the end—and soon we may cross the canal towards home.

Dream that we may all live to meet again . . .

In the daily prayers of your affectionate son,

Kory D. Curcuru

BVG